Death Range

Bullet-scarred Jack Cain figured he was through cleaning up gun-crazy ranges and wild cow towns. He called it a day and headed for Montana to buy a small spread and raise cows. But a hundred miles up-country, ten-year-old Ethan Wilder stepped out of the bushes and told him his ma was badly shot up and near to dying. Would he come take a look?

Barely two hours on Cain was lucky to survive the hail of lead that sizzled out of the rocks right at him. Not only that, what followed that ambush turned out to be Jack Cain's greatest test. The question was . . . would he survive it?

A man could only hope.

Death Range

Elliot Long

A Black Horse Western

ROBERT HALE · LONDON

© Elliot Long 2009
First published in Great Britain 2009

ISBN 978-0-7090-8758-8

Robert Hale Limited
Clerkenwell House
Clerkenwell Green
London EC1R 0HT

www.halebooks.com

Typeset by
Derek Doyle & Associates, Shaw Heath
Printed and bound in Great Britain by
CPI Antony Rowe, Chippenham and Eastbourne

CHAPTER ONE

As Jack Cain topped the crest of the arroyo his horse's ears pricked up. It lifted its head and scented the air. But Cain could tell the moves were more out of curiosity than fear and he felt comforted by that. Nevertheless, he discreetly turned his gaze towards where the horse was staring.

There were cottonwoods and willows down there by the stream, but he could see no movement other than that which was natural. However, he wasn't fooled. The horse was born to this wild country and it was sensitive to its irregularities. Something, or somebody, was moving around down there and he would do well to note it. Cain loosened the retaining loop over the trigger of his Colt .45, but did not draw the weapon from the well-used holster tied to his right thigh. The precaution made, he eased his horse down the long slope to the creek's edge.

He was taking a chance, he knew, and with his experience it was a damned fool thing to do. Nevertheless, some instinct was telling him things weren't that bad so he eased himself out of the saddle and drank of the clear mountain water. A yard or two downstream his roan also slurped its fill.

When his thirst was satisfied Cain filled his canteen. However, he made sure his hand never strayed far from his belt weapon. Twice he heard rustling in the undergrowth, the crack of a twig. It was possible it was some critter foraging for food. It certainly wasn't somebody wanting to ambush him or he would have done it by now. And that opinion posed another question: who, around here, would want to bushwhack him anyway? He was a stranger hereabouts.

When he located the exact place the noises were coming from he spun around, pulling his Colt. It was a smooth, silky movement. He raised his arm and aimed the weapon saying, crisply, 'OK, show yourself.'

Reaction to his order was instant. 'Please, don't shoot, mister!'

It was a boy who came out of the bushes. He was wearing faded denim pants, scuffed-up boots, and a blue, clearly often-washed flannel shirt. His awry blond hair had not seen a comb this day, of that Cain was sure.

The boy was staring up at him with frightened blue eyes. His arms strained to reach high over his head. His round face, Cain noticed, was unusually pale for a boy who must have spent a great deal of his time in the open air. He said, slight harshness in his voice, 'Don't you know better than to creep up on a man, boy?'

'I was trying to figure out if you was a badman, sir,' the boy said.

'If I was, you'd be dead,' Cain said. 'Now, why are you skulking around like this?'

'It's my ma, sir, she's awful sick.' The boy waved a hand towards the west slope of the arroyo. 'Can you come and take a look?'

Irritation flowed through Cain. 'Haven't you got kin to bother with this, boy? I'm on other business.'

'No, sir; they're all dead.'

Cain stared. 'Dead, you say?'

'Yes, sir.'

Cain rubbed his chin thoughtfully. 'I see,' he said. He raised his dark brows. 'Well, you'd better get up here, boy, and we'll go take a look.'

The youngster dropped his arms and Cain bent and gave him assistance by gripping his arm near the shoulder and hoisting him up to land him spread-legged in front of the saddle horn. After the boy's instructions as to which direction to take, Cain urged the roan through the trees and up the opposite side of the arroyo. As he did the boy said,

'Ma's been shot, sir. She's bleeding awful bad.'

Astonished, Cain stared at the back of the boy's head. 'What d'you mean . . . shot?'

'Just like I say, sir,' the boy said.

Cain found that highly irregular, for, in these lawless Western lands, there were still codes of conduct and the killing, wounding or violating of any decent women was, more often than not, a lynching affair. However, the soiled doves were often treated

7

like dirt. He did not approve of such treatment and on occasion demonstrated that fact in no uncertain terms. Nevertheless, he knew most of those fallen angels were more than capable of holding their own. They would likely have derringers hidden about their persons, or knives secreted in their boot-tops. Cain knew they were in no way afraid to use either should the need arise. But to have a *genteel* woman violated . . . now, that was entirely another matter.

'You know how she was shot, boy?' he said.

The lad turned and looked up, his eyes round, his face still ashen. 'Raiders come, sir, but I never saw their faces. They were masked and hid out amongst the rocks near the ranch. Ma was out front.' His lips trembled, but he didn't cry. 'They shot her down like a dog, sir. Just like a dog.'

'Where were you at the time?' Cain said.

'I was in the barn loft moving hay, else I guess they would've shot me, too, if I'd been with Ma.' Cain now saw tears begin to well up into the boy's blue eyes. 'I figured on getting Pa's Winchester out of the house, but by the time I climbed down from the loft and got outside it was all quiet.'

Cain decided right off this was one spunky kid.

'You got a name, son?' he said.

'Ethan Wilder, sir.'

'Ethan, uh?'

'Yes.'

'Just how old are you, boy?'

'Going on ten.'

'And your pa's dead, you say?'

'Yes, sir.'

'And you didn't see the faces of the men who attacked your ma?'

'No, sir, didn't see anything real well, just thought I saw, but I figure I know who they're likely to be.'

Cain said, 'But you ain't full certain?'

'No, sir.'

Cain moved uneasily in his saddle. His feeling of irritation at being drawn into this was not going away, even though the boy was clearly in trouble. God dammit, he was still not fully healed up from the hunk of lead he'd taken the last time he took a hand in cleaning up somebody else's mess, albeit on that occasion he was wearing a badge and getting paid to do it.

The boy was saying, 'I reckon it's got to be Barton Hanson's men, sir. He owns the Bar H. A big spread north of here.'

'Has he been giving you trouble?' Cain said.

'Made no secret of the fact he wants our water,' the boy said. 'And to get it he wants to buy the ranch. We ain't all that big, I guess, so Pa reckoned Hanson considered he could bully us into it, but Pa weren't a man to be pushed into anything he did not want to do. Pa and Mr Hanson had some mighty big arguments, though – that was when Pa was alive, of course.'

'But there was no shooting?' Cain asked.

'No, sir, but Pa got killed, even so; shot down three months ago close to Shoshone Bluffs ... from ambush, was Sheriff Neal Maher's opinion. He's the law over at Eagle Rock. It's got to mean something, ain't it?'

'Did the sheriff bring anybody to justice?' Cain said.

The boy played with the horse's mane. 'No, sir, but he formed a posse. He told Ma he figured it was a single marksman that did the job; he told her he found two shell cases behind a rock about fifty yards from where Pa was gunned down. He said he tried to pick up the man's trail but the son of a bitch – his words, sir – was too clever and got clean away.'

'And nothing's happened since?' Cain said.

The boy said, 'Oh, yes, sir, month later my brother Brian, Texas Jack and Laramie Bob got shot down. Tex and Laramie were Pa's two ranch hands.' The boy shook his head. 'Sheriff Maher didn't catch those killers either, sir. He said he figured five men were in on that ambush. And now Ma's been hit.'

The boy's head went down once more. Cain felt for the boy. His father, his brother and now his mother, shot down in the most brutal of ways. Cain felt sure it would be enough to cripple most people, but he also knew children were resilient, more resilient than they were given credit for. Nevertheless, he still felt keen sympathy for the lad; felt inclined to put his arm around the boy's shoulders to comfort him, and did raise his hand to do so but then dropped it to his side again. A hard life from an early age, in which there had been little comfort after his pa died, made him too hard-shelled to open himself up like that. But come the day and the situation, who knows? He might put on a more human face.

'Anybody else with you on the ranch, apart from you and your ma?' he said.

'Medicine Bow Reynolds, sir; he kind of helps out.'

'Is he one of your hands?' Cain said.

'Just a good friend, sir; he's out on the south range right now, mending fences.'

'I see,' Cain said. 'On the ride here I passed two homesteads in a small valley couple of miles back. Have you got nester trouble?'

Ethan shook his head. 'No, sir; they give us no bother. Pa said they've paid for their land, like we have. But their presence ain't going down too well with those on the range who ain't divvied up.'

'It seldom does,' said Cain. 'Nesters and ranchers don't usually mix, but sooner or later they got to learn how. The West is filling up.'

'That was Pa's view,' Ethan said, 'that's why we gave them no trouble. In fact, Pa helped them settle in, though some of the ranch folk hereabouts didn't like it. Mr Hanson for one.' The boy broke off and looked up. Cain met his blue, pleading stare. 'Can you hurry it up, sir? I'm awful worried about Ma.'

'Figure it's that bad, huh?' Cain said.

'Yes, sir.'

'Very well, boy.' Cain eased the roan into a canter.

Top of the next rise the ground gently sloped down for about a mile. At the bottom of a long, grassy slope, and 200 yards on from where it levelled out, Cain saw a large log ranch house with a shingle

11

roof, two big clapboard barns and a log bunkhouse roofed with sod. Two corrals made of sturdy poles were shaded by cottonwoods. The corrals were a hundred yards north of the buildings, beyond the big vegetable garden at the rear of the house. Cain saw four horses were penned in the corral nearest to the house. The other pen was empty. The broad stream that flowed through the arroyo they had left behind minutes ago was about a quarter of a mile from the ranch. It bent around the west side of the property. And all the way the stream was lined with willows and cottonwoods. It was then that Cain noticed a well was dug at the back of the house. It told him the Wilders were not dependent on the river for water. Maybe they had a pump over the sink in the house, too? It sure looked that kind of place.

The ranch house and its environs were smart and in good repair. Over the years, the boy's father must have invested a deal of sweat and muscle in this place before he took lead – his lady, too, considering the sparkle of the glass in the windows and the neatness of a front garden full of bright blooms of various colours. However, there were signs of neglect, all too accountable if the boy's father, brother and the hired help had so recently died and so violently. He shook his head. Goddamn, it was a hell of a situation he was riding into. It was then that he noticed an odd thing and it caused him to tense up slightly. There was no body lying out front as he'd expected there would be.

'Where's your ma, son?'

'I managed to help her into the house, sir. She's on her bed.'

Cain stared at the boy. More respect for the youngster welled up in him. 'You're getting to be a real man, Ethan,' he said.

'Couldn't leave her out in the dust, sir.'

'No, boy, you couldn't,' Cain said firmly.

But surveying the surrounding countryside warily Cain eased the roan down the long slope through clusters of grazing cattle. At the two-horse tie rail before the white picket fence enclosing the flowerbeds he pulled rein. He saw the dark stain in the dust nearby and he decided it must be the woman's blood.

Cain lifted his gaze and stared beyond the garden. He saw pink roses in full bloom, weaving across the long stoop and also under the shingle-roof of the house. In the left corner of the stoop there was a bench-swing with cushions on it moving lazily in the wildflower-scented breeze blowing in off the big range surrounding the ranch. He narrowed his eyelids. Cold anger filled him. It was too nice a day to have death visiting here, if the lady was dead, that is. However, he also knew the grim reaper was no respecter of time nor place – he came when he was due and he did not give a damn about the misery he left behind.

The boy slid down the horse's withers to the worn ground but Cain climbed down more easily, stiff from being in the saddle since early morning, apart from the brief stop by the creek The boy was running up the path as he looped rein over the hitch rail to the side of the wicket gate.

Cain followed the boy, not knowing what to expect, maybe a dead woman by now. The thought was a chilling one.

He walked through the open front door and stepped into a spacious room. The far wall was adorned with two stuffed antelope heads, and the head of a mountain lion in full snarl. There were spreads of longhorns on all the walls. Various pictures hung on each wall, most of them depicting Western life. On the far wall was a shelf of well-used books. Two Winchester rifles were resting on wooden dowels driven into the same log wall. A shotgun was propped in the angle of the big, rough-hewn yellow-stone fireplace. Logs were glowing on the stone hearth floor. A nice touch was two inglenooks, one on each side the fireplace.

There was a woman's influence everywhere: flower-patterned curtains and peg rugs strewn about on the board floor, fresh blooms in vases. He saw that cushions with knitted covers were plumped up on the cowhide settees and seats. For a moment long-held ambitions welled up in Cain. One day he hoped to have a place like this and a good woman to look after it. One day.

He realized the boy was tugging urgently at his sleeve.

'This way, sir.'

Cain allowed himself to be led down the passage-way that branched off to his left. He found it was

14

lined with other rooms, probably bedrooms. He decided this fine house was not built in a day.

At the second door, which was open, the boy led him into the room. The woman was lying on the bed. She was an attractive, well-formed blonde in her mid-thirties, about in line with his own years. However, it was clear that her face – though at the moment made flour-pale by her injuries – was hardened by years of uncompromising life on this wild frontier. Even so, Cain noticed there was tenderness in her expression, too, which, he reckoned, would always be there, whatever life elected to throw at her. Blood soaked her plain white blouse and blue skirt, as well as the sheets under her. The boy went to her side. 'Ma? I've got help for you like I said I would.'

The woman moved, moaned but went quiet again. Now by her side it became clear to Cain that the woman was unconscious, or close to it, and that her moan was probably just an instinctive maternal reaction to her son's voice. Cain studied her. What appeared to be a large exit wound was at the top of her right shoulder. A thin pad of blood-soaked cotton material was laid on it. Had the woman managed to patch the wound up while the boy went for help?

He leaned forward. The wound was too close to the big vein in her throat for comfort. It was a terrible injury, made, Cain suspected, by a heavy-calibre bullet. He bent over the woman and spoke into her ear. 'If you can hear me, ma'am, I'm going to have to turn you to ascertain how bad your wound is. Is that all right with you?' Only her eyelids fluttered.

Cain turned her as gently as he could. She groaned and whimpered a little. It looked as though the bullet had entered her side, glanced off a rib and tracked up the inside of her shoulder blade and out where he first sighted the wound. It appeared there were no vital organs damaged. But there had clearly been initial heavy loss of blood. However, it seemed the flow had eased some time ago. And that was a consolation: he would not have to dig for the bullet. That would be a situation he would not relish. But if there were the need to do so he would not shirk the responsibility. Lead, he knew, if it was not removed, could poison the system, enough to kill. How he knew was from bitter experience. His pa died because there was nobody to dig out the Arapaho bullet that was buried deep in his side. Some said poison might have been on it. Arapahos did that to their bullets sometimes, or so rumour had it. However, nobody ruled out lead poisoning, either.

Cain closed his eyes. Though it was a long time ago he vividly recalled the event of his father's death. The Arapaho trapped them fifteen miles north of the Smokey Hill River. Pa and he holed up and managed to fight them off, but in the process Pa took lead. Cain set his strong chin into a thin, bitter line. He had been only twelve years old at the time. He did not know how important it was to dig lead out of a wound and his pa could not tell him because he was rambling with the fever most of the time. When he did eventually get his pa to the Overland way station on Crow Creek three days later, the men there did their best to save him but they came to the conclusion it was too late. The awful thing was, his pa's dying took a week and the last two agonized days near shattered him. His pa was all he had left in the world. Being alone in the West at his age was not a thing to relish. It did make a man of him very quickly, but a cold unyielding man in many ways. However, it also left him with a keen sense of justice, and a need to help the less fortunate until they could help themselves.

He said to the boy, 'Where does your ma keep her bed linen, son?'

The boy went to the nearby chest of drawers and with some difficulty pulled open the middle drawer of the three. Cain went with him and lifted out a large white cotton sheet and tore it into bandages. Some of the sheet he saved to make a thicker pad for the exit wound. Then he went back to the woman and said, 'Going to have to take off your clothes, ma'am.'

She didn't move; didn't even flicker an eyelid. She was clearly deeply out of it and that, decided Cain, was to the good.

He worked quickly but carefully, getting the boy to help him. Soon the woman was undressed and the wound was cleaned and bandaged. She groaned a couple of times during the process but did not wake up. Now Cain decided he needed to get her out of the soiled bed and between the clean sheets of

17

another one. After that, allow her to come out of her unconsciousness naturally.

He bent over her and lifted her as gently as he could. He was surprised she was so light.

'Lead me to another bed, boy,' he said.

Ethan, clearly relieved that his ma was being tended to said, eagerly, 'Yes, sir.' Then his look turned to one of anxious pleading. 'She's going to be all right, isn't she, sir?'

'I truly hope so, boy,' Cain said, but felt he could add no more to that. He did not want to build up false hopes in the youngster. The wound would need proper medical treatment. Now he felt like a caged lion. It looked as though he'd ridden into a hornet's nest here. Worse, it looked as though he would have to stay here until he considered it was reasonably safe to leave the boy. He could not just ride away and leave the boy to his own devices. It wasn't in him. There must be friends to take up the responsibility? Such as this Medicine Bow Reynolds the boy spoke about. Cain rubbed his chin. But if he did stay it would sure mess up his plans. He was finished with the likes of what appeared to be happening here. He wanted to be away from it all, wanted some peace – a quiet valley in Montana to settle and raise cattle on like he'd planned to do for so long. He did not want to be mixed up in this kind of lunacy any more, keeping kill-crazy, land-hungry bastards apart. Yet there was another part of him saying yes he should and that angered him more than somewhat.

18

He looked out of the glazed window, across the rolling rangeland. What the hell was he getting himself into?

CHAPTER TWO

After transferring the woman to the bed in the room next to the one she was in, Cain now stood in the big common room rubbing his chin. The best thing he could do now was to get a doctor to Mrs Wilder and find someone to look after the boy.

He looked down at Ethan, who was standing next to him. 'What's the name of that town you mentioned a while ago, boy?'

'Eagle Rock.'

'Do they have a doctor there?'

'Yes, sir.'

'Is it far?'

'Pa claimed around ten miles.'

Cain nodded. 'I see. Guess I'm going to have to ride to there, son, to fetch that sawbones. Will you be all right with that? I mean, leaving you here alone for a while?'

'I'll be all right, sir. I've done it before.'

The faint beat of hoofs outside stopped any more

talk and Cain looked down at the boy. 'Any ideas as to who it could be?'

Ethan frowned and shook his head. 'Medicine Bow is not due back until tomorrow. Like I said, he's mending fences down the south pasture. Been broken down again. We've lost maybe a hundred head one way and another because of it. It's got to be cow-thieves is Medicine Bow's opinion.' Ethan rubbed his nose as if he was speculating on a possibility. 'It could be Medicine Bow but I figure it sounds like there is more than one rider, sir.'

Cain nodded. 'I reckon you've got your figuring about right, boy.' He tapped his lips with a finger, thoughtfully. 'You mentioned rustler trouble just now. What's this Sheriff Maher you talked of doing about it . . . anything?'

'He says he's investigating.'

'Investigating, uh?' *Not very well*, Cain decided. He added, 'You also talked about wire being used on this range.'

'Yes, sir; most folks have it.'

'But not all.'

'No, sir, one or two don't like it. King Laker for one. He owns the Floating L, out near Bear Creek.'

Cain rubbed his chin. 'Uh-huh.'

Ethan shuffled and looked uneasily at the stout door. 'I figure to get me a gun, sir,' he said. 'I ain't happy about this.'

As he was speaking Ethan was already making for the shotgun Cain had noticed when he first entered the house, leaning in the corner by the huge yellow-stone fireplace. The boy picked it up, broke it and checked it for shells. He snapped it shut. Clearly, it was fully loaded. Cain noted that the gun was near as big as Ethan. Cain narrowed his eyelids. Not doubt about it: when this boy was grown he would be a man to ride the river with.

Cain drew his Colt .45, a smooth, practised lift. He eased up to the door and peered carefully out, around the jamb. He saw three riders were coming at a fast clip down the long slope. Cattle were scattering before them. A minute later they pulled up before the picket fence, near the gate. The tall one in the broadcloth suit and white Stetson was a well-built, powerful-looking man with square brick-red features set into hard, determined lines. Long grey hair hung down from under his Stetson and curled into the nape of his neck.

Not dismounting he called,

'Jane Wilder?'

Cain stepped out on to the gallery, Colt held down by his right thigh. The boy came with him, holding the shotgun in two hands.

Cain said, 'She's indisposed.'

The two riders, one each side of the big man, were rangemen, that was clear, and were dressed in working range gear. One was a short man with a round weather-beaten face and dark, restless eyes. He wore his Colt in the cross-draw position. The other was a tall beanpole of a man with a scrawny neck and a large Adam's apple. A vivid white scar ran down the right side of his face, giving him an ugly look. His lips were thick and pliable and the scar that continued across those lips distorted them enough to make him appear as though he was constantly sneering. An ivory-handled Colt .45 hung on his left thigh, housed in a worn holster. A slouch hat sat jammed down on his narrow head.

The most powerful-looking man of the three was obviously the leader. He stuck out his deeply cleft chin and leaned forward aggressively. Cain met his hard brown stare head on.

The man said, 'What the hell is that supposed to mean . . . indisposed?'

Cain shrugged. 'Like I said.'

'You mean she's sick?'

'Kind of.'

The big man's look turned belligerent. 'What sort of answer is that . . . and just who the hell are you, mister?'

'Mind if I turn that around?' Cain said. 'Just who the hell are *you*?'

Before the man could answer, the boy blurted, 'It's Barton Hanson, sir. Him as owns the Bar H, like I explained.'

'The one who wants your ranch and water?' Cain said.

'Yes, sir.'

Cain turned to the big rancher and smiled faintly. 'In that case, from what the boy has told me, you're not welcome here, Hanson, so just turn your horse around and ride out and things will be fine.'

The Bar H owner glared; a deep scowl formed on

his broad forehead. 'I'm not used to be being talked to like that, mister. Now put that gun up and step aside before this gets out of hand. This is between Mrs Wilder and me and no damned business of yours.'

Cain said, 'I'm making it my business.'

Barton Hanson's glare became even fiercer. He was obviously struggling to hold down his anger. He rested hard hands on the saddle horn. 'Fellow, you're making this mighty difficult for me.'

Cain shrugged. 'No difficultly, Hanson, just ride out.'

The Bar H rancher's displeasure was clearly reaching its peak. He leaned forward, his brow forming a fleshy overhang above his eyes. He said, 'Let me give you some advice: back out of this. I'm here to see Jane Wilder and, sure as hell, I'm through talking to you.'

'That's odd,' Cain said, 'I've got the same thing in mind . . . through talking, that is.'

The Bar H owner leaned back in the saddle, a furious scowl on his brick-red face. He waved a beefy paw at his two henchmen and barked, 'Deal with the son of a bitch, I don't care how. Break his goddamn arm or something.'

Cain lifted his already drawn Colt. With swift, fluid movement he armed the weapon on its way up from his side. Without hesitation he levelled the weapon and pressed the trigger. Only a split second had elapsed. Hanson's fine white Stetson sailed off his head to land in the dust twelve or more feet to his rear. His two henchmen, their faces a mix of alarm and surprise, froze in mid-move, their hands hovering over gun butts.

The middle-aged one of the two turned his head.

'Boss?' He clearly wanted to know what to do next.

Before the Bar H owner could answer Cain said, 'Hear me, Hanson, go any further with this and the next one will finish it.'

Hanson's irises were like two brownstone pebbles, hard and round, but Cain saw no fear in them. The Bar H owner said, 'You know if you shoot me my boys will get you.'

'But you'll be first,' Cain said, 'and the rest remains in doubt.'

He armed his Colt again, keeping the weapon aimed at Hanson's now bare forehead. The rancher continued to stare, as if he was now weighing up a bad situation. After moments he said,

'How would you like to work for me, mister?'

Surprised, Cain said, 'I'm not for sale.'

'I pay top wages,' Hanson said.

'The answer's still the same.'

The ranch owner eased back in his saddle and said, 'All right, then at least tell me what you're doing here, and why Jane Wilder can't come to the door to speak for herself.'

Ethan blurted, 'Because you shot her, that's why.' To emphasize his words the boy hefted up the shotgun, but Cain put his hand on the dull blue steel of the barrels and kept them pointed at the boards of the stoop floor. Then he grinned disarmingly at the

Bar H owner. 'That's how the boy told it, Hanson; what have you got to say about that?'

The Bar H owner stared, clearly amazed. 'Why, that's crazy.' He looked down at the boy. 'Ethan, it don't do to lie, you hear?'

'I ain't lying!' Ethan said. 'You were behind those rocks!' He pointed to the cluster of boulders to the south, which formed a base around a yellow-stone bluff, which was maybe forty feet in height.

Hanson growled and seemed to take time to calm himself. When he was settled he aimed his stare at Cain and said, 'OK, you'd better tell me what the boy's told you, and, while you're doing it, I'd still like to know where you fit into this.'

Cain decided it was a reasonable request. He told all that had happened up until the time Hanson and his men appeared on the scene. However, he did not disclose the reasons why he got involved. The hell of it was, he wasn't quite sure himself – it just seemed the right thing to do.

When he was finished Hanson said, 'And you tended to Mrs Wilder's wound?'

'Uh-huh.'

Hanson screwed up his eyelids and adopted his aggressive lean forward once more. 'So, what do you aim to do now . . . ride on?'

Cain pursed his lips. 'I haven't quite made my mind up yet. The first thing I need to do is to ride into Eagle Rock to get the sawbones to Mrs Wilder, but it's awkward just now.'

Hanson said, 'Awkward. . . ?'

Cain nodded. 'Meaning, I don't like leaving the boy and the woman alone here after what has happened.'

Hanson eased back in the saddle. Abruptly, he turned to the middle-aged puncher at his right side. 'Ned, ride into Eagle Rock and get Doc Mailer out here. Call on Sheriff Maher, too. Acquaint him with the facts.'

Ned Sullivant nodded and without comment turned his horse and went up the trail heading west, across this huge range that was emerald-green with tall new grass and full of colour, made by the reds of Indian paintbrush and the yellows of rubeckia, as well as a host of other flowers.

Cain became aware Hanson was eyeing him up. 'Will that do?'

'Do for me,' Cain said.

'Can I see her now?' Hanson said.

Cain shook his head. 'She's sleeping. No point.' And Ethan added, 'And I ain't letting you see her, nohow.'

Barton Hanson stared sourly at Ethan. 'Boy, you're too much like your father,' he said, 'stubborn to the point of foolishness.' He swung his gaze back on to Cain and added, 'Mister, if it'll ease your thinking on this, I didn't kill Wilder or his son Brian, or any of his boys, and I didn't wound Jane Wilder.'

'If you say so,' Cain said.

Hanson scowled. 'Dammit, I do say.'

'Seems to me you're trying a little too hard to make your point, Hanson,' Cain said. 'Sometimes

DEATH RANGE

that can suggest a guilty man.'

Hanson's craggy face once more became belligerent. 'By God, you'd better start watching your
tongue, mister, I ain't used to being talked to like
this.'

Cain said, 'That's too bad.'

Barton Hanson growled. He sat silent on his big
chestnut for long moments, glaring with those
brown, hard eyes. Then he tilted his chin. 'OK,' he
said, 'you've done your good deed for the day, now
let me repeat my advice: ride on; you don't know
what you're letting yourself for.'

'And you do?'

Hanson said, his stare stony once more, 'Read it
how you will, mister.'

Again Cain offered him a faint smile. 'Thing is,
Hanson, I'm getting to feel I just can't ride on. I'm
fast coming round to liking this country.'

Hanson raised dark brows and sat back heavily in
the saddle. 'All right, I've said my piece. Now, when
Ned Sullivant gets back with Doc Mailer, tell him to
head back to the Bar H.' He sat for moments, sucking his lower lip before he added, 'I'll send over
Lodge Woman to tend to Jane's needs until she is
well again. And tell Jane we still need to talk when
she's well.'

'Maybe she won't want to talk to you,' Cain said,
but then conceded, 'As for your offer of a nurse . . .
well, that's good of you, Hanson.'

The Bar H rancher nodded. Without further
comment he turned to the beanpole rider beside

28

him. Cain was close enough to the man to realize he had a big problem with body odour. 'Jake Mole, get my hat,' Hanson said.

'Sure, boss.'

The lean puncher climbed down, retrieved the Stetson, handed it to Hanson and then remounted. Barton Hanson poked his finger through the holes and stared hard at Cain, then placed the hat over his long grey locks. Without another word he swung his big roan around. He galloped off past the bunch of rocks at the base of what Ethan said had been the ambush butte, then crossed the stream. The tall beanpole rider joined him. Together they rode at a fast lick through the willows and cottonwoods and out towards the green, wooded hills in the near distance.

Cain watched them go. He holstered his Colt, his thoughts reluctant. Judging from what he'd heard and seen up to now this range was kill-crazy. Four dead that he knew of. Even worse, there was a woman badly injured in the ranch house behind him and close to dying.

He became aware that the boy was tugging at his coat sleeve. When he looked down into the boy's face he saw pleading there. 'Now pa's gone I want you to stay, sir. Will you do that?'

Cain rested his hand on the boy's shoulder. 'I regret to say it isn't as easy as that, boy; but I'll give it some thought. By the way, who's this Lodge Woman Hanson talked about?'

The boy seemed to accept his words and said,

'She's a Crow squaw. She cooks for Mr Hanson and helps about the house. She's a medicine woman as well.'

Cain said, 'Ain't there a Mrs Hanson?'

'No, sir; she died of the influenza afore I was born, so Ma told me.'

'I see.'

Cain rubbed his chin. Oddly, despite Ethan's condemnation of him, he was beginning to have mixed feelings about Barton Hanson. On the one hand Hanson's offers of help were generous ones. Yet, on the other hand, Cain found he held niggling doubts that the deeds were genuine. Minutes ago, Hanson was prepared to have Jack Cain's arm broken, or worse.

He patted Ethan on the shoulder and said, 'OK, son, go see how your ma is and put that shotgun back where it belongs. Last thing I want is for you to shoot your goddamned leg off.'

Ethan gave him a broad grin, dramatically altering his, up to now, unhappy face. He said, 'Yes, sir, but don't let Ma hear you cussing like that.'

Cain returned the smile and ruffled Ethan's blond hair. 'I'll be sure to bear that in mind.'

He watched the boy go over the threshold, then he stabled his horse in the barn closest to the house. He groomed it and fed it oats from the galvanized bin close by the four stalls built into the barn.

He was returning to the house when the whirr of disturbed air whispered past his left ear. Almost simultaneously it was followed by the crack of a rifle, which sent echoes squabbling across the range. Dust jetted up ten feet ahead him. The closeness of it set him running for cover.

CHAPTER THREE

Cain was running and weaving like a mad thing by the time the next shot came and missed. However, he had the presence of mind to establish that the bullets were coming from the bluff Ethan said his ma's ambusher had fired from. The third shot also missed him and plumed up dust ahead.

Cain jumped the picket fence enclosing the front garden with one long-legged stride and ran across the flower-beds into the house. There he did not hesitate. He made for the rifles racked on the wall. He lifted one down. He checked it was loaded and jacked a shell into the breech. At that moment Ethan came running in from the bedrooms, his eyelids round with concern.

'Who is doing the shooting, sir?'

'That's what I aim to find out, boy. Now, just get a hold on that shotgun and stay close here and look out for your ma. Can you do that?'

Ethan's blue eyes were lit with eager determination. 'You can trust me, sir. They won't get anywhere near my ma, you see.'

Cain looked down at the spunky youngster, grinned and ruffled his hair. 'Know something, boy? I'm inclined to believe you. *Now get to it.*'

He went out of the door crouching low, rifle in hand. He bounded across the stoop and through the colourful flower-beds. The rifle cracked again: one, two, three times, sending harsh echoes ricocheting across the range. Behind Cain heard lead *thunk* into the logs of the house front.

Now over the white picket fence he weaved across the intervening space between the house and the nearest barn. Moments later he raced into its cover and leaned against the weathered boards, breathing hard. His thinking soon got into gear. He needed to get into those rocks at the bottom of the bluff. Above all, he needed to know who was doing the shooting. He also wanted to know if it was the same son of a bitch who'd shot Jane Wilder, for, strangely, he did not buy Ethan's claim that it was Hanson and his boys, even though he held suspicions it might have been. Maybe, being alone and scared, Ethan's young mind just ran riot.

Cain padded down the side of the barn, hardly daring to breathe. At the corner of the building he eased up to its angle and carefully peered around its edge. The jumble of rocks at the foot of the forty-foot high bluff revealed themselves one by one. Almost right off he saw the glint of sun on metal, the hint of the top of a steeple hat above the low rocks on the rim of the butte.

Cain pulled the rifle into his shoulder and jacked off two shots fast. He watched gritty dust flare off the rock. As he hoped, Steeple Hat ducked and disappeared below the rim of the butte with some alacrity.

Sure as a man could be, Cain decided the fellow must now be seeking fresh cover. Using that assumption he sprinted across the ground between the barn and the rocks at the foot of the butte. As he ran Cain found one requirement drumming in his brain: he needed to take this bastard alive; he needed to make him sing even though, rationally thinking, Jack Cain should be riding out of here and to hell with what was going on because it was none of his damned business.

But when a man takes shots at you. . . . He began to make his way up though the rocks ignoring the dryness in his mouth and the increased thumping of his heart. Halfway up the butte, he dislodged pebbles and Steeple Hat bobbed up, yards from his last hideout.

Cain crouched as lead sang off the rocks, throwing up powder and splinters. But the strikes were at least ten feet away. Cain reckoned, after Steeple Hat missed so badly just now, that he did not earn his living as a bushwhacker, or had only recently taken up that murderous profession. Either way, the son of a Mexican bitch was not going to last long in that line of work on this showing.

Cain straightened up and fired three shots. One

bullet ricocheted off into the blue sky, directly in line with the bushwhacker's hideout. The other two sprayed up dust and splinters close to the bush-whacker. The volley was enough to make the son of a bitch duck down.

Using the interlude Cain shifted further to his right and once more began climbing. A couple of minutes later he topped out and bellied up to one of the rocks littering the top of the butte. Then, with great caution, he peered across the rough surface of the butte's summit. Steeple Hat, he saw, was crouched behind a large boulder, rifle sighted up ready to fire. He was staring anxiously across and down the walls of the butte, apparently not inter-ested in what was happening on the summit. *Amigo*, Cain thought, with some comfort, *that isn't the place to look.*

A tight smile formed on his lips. He estimated the distance between the two of them was about fifty yards. He couldn't be better placed to take that murderous son of a Mexican bitch alive. He stood up and lined up the Winchester and hoped the man understood some English. 'Stay real still, mister, and drop your rifle.'

Steeple Hat spun and fired in one rapid move-ment. But because of his haste and his apparent inaccuracy previously, the lead went wide and Cain, never a man to rush a shot, aimed coolly and trig-gered with precision. The man yelled and staggered back, his arms spread wide as he hit the boulder behind him. His steeple hat jarred off his head revealing greasy black hair. Cain saw blood was already staining the top of his left shoulder. The gore was spreading rapidly, crimsoning his fancy shirt. It would be a painful wound, Cain knew, but would not be lethal unless it became infected. Even so, Cain hoped it would be enough to make this son of old Mexico think twice before risking another shot.

He thought wrong. The bastard came off the rock fast; his face wild and twisted. He began firing rapidly. Cain felt lead pluck at his leather vest. Another bullet clipped his right earlobe, sending pain spurting through him and causing blood to drip on to the collar of his green shirt.

Knowing now he could no longer take any chances with this crazy son of a Mexican puta, Cain jacked off two shots. He saw blood sprout redly on the man's chest. The fellow slammed back against the yellow boulder behind him. Then he bent over and began coughing blood, which gushed out of his mouth and splattered on to the rough rocky top of the butte. Then he looked up. His eyes held a sad, spaniel-like look of disappointment, which reached across the intervening space to Cain. After moments he said, as if he was profoundly surprised,

'You have killed me, gringo.'

Cain stared, his anger hot. 'You killed yourself, dammit. I wanted to talk.'

The Mexican said, 'You did not say.'

At that moment the greaser had the temerity to die.

Still watchful, Cain walked up to the lifeless form while pressing his handkerchief to his bleeding earlobe. He felt inclined to kick the son of a bitch to vent his anger further but held off and studied him instead. Steeple Hat wore all Mexican gear: short bolero jacket with plenty of silver adorning it, frilled shirt and velveteen pants, with the inner legs lined with leather and split into flares at their bottoms. The trousers were also decorated with silver. A pearl-handled Colt was in its tooled holster on his right hip. Shells glistened in the loops of his near-full scrolled gun belt. The Winchester rifle was still clasped in his lifeless hand.

A search of his pockets revealed five hundred-dollar bills. Cain rubbed his chin. Was that what his life was worth, and maybe Jane Wilder's? On the other hand who would want Jack Cain's life on this range? He was a complete stranger here. It didn't make sense.

Cain stared without feeling at the cadaver. He must have a name. And, if he operated locally, the boy would likely know it.

Cain grabbed the back of the Mexican's collar. With ease he dragged him to the edge of the bluff and tossed his carcass down the forty-foot drop to land with a bony crunch against the boulders at the bottom of it. Then he made a meticulous search of the rest of the bluff top, looking for shell cases . . . ones different from those strewn around the place where the Mexican had lain in wait for him. Those were .44 Winchester hulls. Considering the severity

37

of Jane Wilder's wound he was reasonably sure that the bullet that hit her came from a higher-calibre weapon.

After some searching he found what he was looking for. The shell case suggested it came from a Spencer .50 rifle. Just one. There was confidence for you. The bastard must have been sure one would be enough to put Jane Wilder's lights out. He could only hope the bastard thought wrong.

Cain pocketed the case and climbed down after the body of the Mexican. At the base of the butte he grabbed the greaser's not too clean collar and dragged him across the flat, worn ground to the picket fence. There he called,

'Ethan?'

After moments the boy came to the door, his face eager. 'Yes, sir?'

'You bothered by the sight of a dead body, boy?'

Ethan shook his head. 'No, sir; I seen Pa and my brother and our two hands when they were dead.'

'In that case come here.'

When Ethan walked through the wicket gate he stared at the Mexican's body with hardly a sign that the sight disturbed him in any way.

'D'you know him, boy?' Cain said.

'Yes, sir, that's Jesus Lopez. He rides for the Lazy R.'

'The Lazy R?'

'Yes, sir.'

Ethan pointed to a range of green hills about fifteen miles away across the undulating range. 'In

38

the Wisher Hills, Matt Wilson owns it. Small spread. He runs a passel of horses on it to sell to the army.'

Cain said, 'Has he been giving you trouble?'

Ethan shook his head. 'No, sir; Pa always considered him to be a friend.'

Cain rubbed his darkly bristled chin. 'I see. Well now, I find that curious. By the way, Ethan, what was the name of that 'puncher Hanson sent to get Doc Mailer just now?'

'Ned Sullivant.'

'Sullivant, huh?'

'Yes.'

Long-reaching recollection threaded searching veins through lawman Cain's memory banks. It was rumoured a fellow called Ned Sullivant once rode with the Reno boys – John, Frank, Slim and Bill – before the Pinkerton Agency hunted them down and brought them to justice in 1866, only to have a party of vigilantes drag the boys out of jail to lynch them. Sullivant must have been mighty young at the time – if it was the same Sullivant – and he must have escaped the noose. Perhaps the brutal lynching of the Reno brothers frightened Sullivant enough to spur him to reform his character. Cain knew such things did occur. However, Cain also possessed a sceptical mind, amply nurtured by ten years of more than often unrewarding law enforcement. It made him firmly of the opinion that hardcases were hardcases and they seldom changed their spots.

The beat of distant hoofs interrupted his ruminations and he found himself more than a little irritated by this second intrusion. He stared, hard anger in his gaze, up the rise in the trail leading to Eagle Rock.

CHAPTER FOUR

Seconds later, comfortable in the saddle on his roan, Ned Sullivant came loping into view. The Bar H 'puncher was accompanying a small buggy in which a huge man was sitting, reins and a small whip in hand. They came to a stop close to the wicket gate where Cain and Ethan were standing, watching them approach. Sullivant waved a hand to the fat man in the buggy.

'This here's Doc Mailer,' he said.

The fat man grunted. He was all of twenty stone, Cain estimated. It was difficult to guess his age, but under his black hat his brown hair was greying at the temples and laughter lines creased the corners of his eyes. The rest of his skin, Cain observed, was almost cherubic in texture. Maybe around forty-five years of age was Cain's best guess.

The sawbones wheezed down from the buggy, the springs groaning at the punishment they were receiving. The black mare in the shafts looked relieved at being temporarily relieved of her burden.

Doc Mailer took a weight out of the bottom of the buggy, attached it to the horse's bridle and dropped it to the ground. After that he picked up his obligatory black bag, turned and levelled his fat-lined grey eyes on the carcass of Jesus Lopez. He stared at Cain.

'Are you in the habit of leaving dead bodies lying around, sir?'

'He will be dealt with,' Cain said brusquely. He turned to Ned Sullivant. With his left hand motioned to the Mexican. 'Know anything about him?'

Sullivant shrugged his shoulders. 'His name's Jesus Lopez, real good with horses, or was, by the look of him. Most ranchers hereabout have used him one time or another to break in new horse stock, mustangs and the like.' Sullivant screwed up his eyelids to give his round face a questioning appearance. 'How come he's dead?'

'He tried using me for target practice,' Cain said. 'Not a good idea.'

Sullivant nodded. 'Uh-huh.' He spat tobacco juice to the ground and appraised Cain. He saw a tall, rangy figure with a hawkish, aquiline face. A fellow who was clad in brown corduroy pants and a plain blue but, at the moment, bloodstained cotton shirt, and a worn leather vest, open at the front. Sullivant took particular note of the Colt that was nestled in the oiled holster at Cain's thigh. He came to the conclusion that this man was, more than likely, one mean *hombre*. He raised his gaze and met Cain's grey stare. 'Well, seeing what I'm seeing right now, I guess that wasn't the wisest thing for Lopez to do.'

Cain nodded. 'You'd better believe it.'

'Oh, I do,' Sullivant said. It was more of a sneer.

Doc Mailer said, a little impatiently, 'This is all very well, but what is far more important is the patient. Where is Mrs Wilder?'

Cain turned to the boy. 'Take the doc to your ma, Ethan.'

Eagerly, the boy said, 'Yes, sir.'

Doc Mailer followed the scuttling lad up the path and into the house. As he did Ned Sullivant said, waving a hand at the silent Lopez, 'What d'you aim to do with him now you've settled his hash?'

'Take him to the Lazy R,' Cain said. 'It'll be Matt Wilson that'll need to dig his grave and put his name on the headboard, for, sure as hell, it isn't going to be me. Top of that, Wilson has got some serious questions to answer.'

Ned Sullivant nodded. 'Serious is right.'

Cain could not make up his mind whether Sullivant was being neighbourly or serious or mocking. He said, 'What d'you know about Wilson, Sullivant?'

'That is for you to find out, is my reckoning,' Sullivant said.

The Bar H 'puncher's amber gaze was neither friendly nor unfriendly; it just lacked communication. Nevertheless, Cain found himself needled by the weak response. He said, 'All right, if that's the way you want it. By the way, Hanson wants you back at the ranch soon as you're through here.' Cain's grey stare hardened to tempered steel. 'And right now I'd say you're through.'

Sullivant shrugged. 'I'm easy with that,' he said. 'Now, mister, I got a question for you: how come you know my name? Because knowing sure gives me title to know yours.'

'Jack Cain.'

Surprise filled Sullivant's features. 'Yeah, *Sheriff* Cain; a mean man with a gun they say. Still County range war, wasn't it? You cleaned up there?'

Cain just stared.

Sullivant held Cain's level gaze for moments then touched the rim of his low-crowned hat with a rope-scarred finger. He smiled. 'Yeah, figured I'd got it right. Well, so long, *Sheriff* Cain.' With that the Bar H 'puncher turned his horse and cantered off towards the hills, not giving him a backward glance.

Cain stared after him, rubbing the place where Jacob Creed's bullet tore through his chest three months ago. The wound had been severe enough to put him in bed for three weeks. It had been a further six weeks to convalesce. Even now he was not one hundred per cent fit. The consensus of opinion in town at the time was unanimous . . . he was lucky to be alive.

He reached for his makings, rolled and lit the cigarette, inhaled and contemplated the fine country spreading around him. Mountains, hills and grass in abundance. A man could settle here very easily. He knew cows, he possessed a nest egg and he was also blessed with enough business nous to make a real go of buying land, building up a spread and running it

44

and it did not necessarily have to be in Montana.

He ground the butt of his finished cigarette into the dust with the sole of his dusty left boot. Fifteen minutes later Doc Mailer came wheezing out of the ranch house. Ethan followed close behind.

On reaching the buggy Doc Mailer unhitched the weight tethering the horse and placed it back in the well of the buggy, along with his bulky black bag. Grunting, he climbed abroad. The vehicle sagged precariously to one side. Seated and with the light whip in his hand he looked down and said, 'The wound is a severe one and needed closing at the exit. I have done the best I can with it but recovery is now in the hands of God' – he smiled – 'along with a little help from me, of course. I have also left a sedative to help her sleep and laudanum to ease the pain.'

Cain said, 'How bad is she, Doc?'

Doc Mailer looked at the boy for some moments, as if making up his mind whether Ethan was old enough to know, then he said, 'Mrs Wilder is a very sick woman, Mr Cain, but she will recover, always providing infection does not set in.' Mailer raised dark brows and leaned forward, as if confidentially. 'However, I do not consider the nursing of a woman to be a man's job.' He played with the reins, coughed and added, 'Particularly a stranger, no offence is intended. However, there is a woman in Eagle Rock upon whom I can call to come out and care for Jane's needs while she heals up. There will be a fee, of course.'

Ethan said, 'Barton Hanson is sending over Lodge Woman.'

Doc Mailer turned his gaze on to the boy with some surprise. He seemed to chew on the information for several moments before he said, 'Well, Lodge Woman is capable enough . . . for an Indian.' He heaved a sigh and stared at Cain. 'Very well, we will leave it at that. I'll visit Mrs Wilder around this time tomorrow. Now, I'll bid you good day, sir.' He turned his gaze on to the boy now. 'And goodbye to you, too, Ethan.'

'Goodbye, sir.'

Doc Mailer clicked at the black in the shafts, turned the buggy on to the worn trail and sent it towards the undulating grasslands and Eagle Rock. When Mailer was over the knoll a couple of hundred yards from the ranch house Cain looked down at Ethan. He said, 'When Lodge Woman comes, boy, I intend to head out to the Lazy R to deliver Lopez. You OK with that?'

'Yes. I get along with Lodge Woman.'

Cain said, 'You know her?'

'Yes. She visits with Ma.'

Cain raised brows in surprise. 'Is that so?'

Ethan said, 'A lot of folks don't cotton to Lodge Woman, but Ma doesn't mind. She says she is interested in the indig . . . indi . . . Indians, sir.'

Cain said, 'Indigenous is the word you're looking for, boy.'

'Yes, sir.'

Cain narrowed his eyelids. For sure, Jane Wilder sounded like an interesting woman. And Lodge Woman sounded interesting, too.

It was mid-afternoon when Lodge Woman rode into the precincts of the Flying W, the Wilder ranch brand name. Cain, meanwhile – figuring it would help the boy take his mind off things – was helping Ethan finish off moving the hay in the barn loft. They did not hear her arrive, which on reflection, Cain decided, was careless. But he did keep his Winchester close.

Lodge Woman eased the big brown mule she was riding to a stop by the garden gate and hollered, 'Who there in house, huh?'

Cain made his way out of the barn and across to where Lodge Woman was sitting her mule. Ethan followed. When Lodge Woman saw them she climbed down. Cain looked at a plump, shapeless woman in a black voluminous ankle-length skirt and black blouse. A silver-studded belt was around her waist. Her hair was shiny and raven-dark. It was parted in the middle and gathered in the nape of her neck and tied with a blue ribbon before it formed a plaited pigtail. Her face was flat and deep bronze. Her eyes were large, dark, luminous and searching when they looked at you. Cain figured she was in middle age, but it was hard to tell. She was carrying a large bag. It appeared to be heavy but she didn't seem prepared to let him take it off her to carry into the house when he offered to. For long moments she stared down at Jesus Lopez's body then looked up and said,

'Him dead, huh?'

'Yes.'

'You kill him?'

'Yes.'

'Huh.' Her dark gaze flicked over him appraisingly before it meet his own. 'You take mule into barn, mister, and feed him?'

Cain nodded. 'I'll do that.'

'You got name?' Lodge Woman said. She waved a hand. 'I know Ethan, son of Jane Wilder, but I don't know you.'

'Jack Cain.'

Lodge Woman grunted. 'Cain plenty good man, I know, I see. Cain make plenty babies when time comes, Lodge Woman know that, too. Now, where is Jane Wilder?'

'In the house.'

'Doc Mailer been?'

'Yes.'

Lodge Woman grunted again. 'Him leave medicine?'

'Yes.'

Lodge Woman walked toward the house, Ethan following. Halfway up the path she turned and said,

'Make sure look after mule good, huh, Jack Cain?'

'I will.'

'Huh.'

Lodge Woman went into the house, followed by Ethan.

Cain took hold of the plaited rawhide hackamore on the mule. He noted the beast was sweating and walked it around to cool it down before he turned to lead it towards the nearest barn. At that moment

Ethan came out of the house, hollered to him and came running. Up close the boy said, 'Lodge Woman don't want me around just now so I'll look after the mule, sir, seeing as you want to ride to the Lazy R.'

Cain looked keenly at the youngster. He said, 'Well, that's helpful, boy. What's Lodge Woman doing?'

'Throwing out Doc Mailer's medicine and preparing herbs.'

'You happy with that?'

'I know Lodge Woman, so does Ma,' Ethan said. 'Like I say, she visits with Ma. Ma and Lodge Woman get on well. They talk for hours. Ma's always been interested in the Indians and their medicines. She'll approve, I think.'

Cain nodded. 'Well, let's hope so.'

He went into the barn. Ethan followed, leading the mule. While Cain saddled up his roan Ethan tended the long-eared beast. Cain was tightening the girth on his roan when he said, 'I'll need a horse to carry Lopez's carcass, son. All right to take one from the corral?'

The boy said, 'Take the bay. He won't give you much trouble when you tie the body on to him.'

Cain nodded. 'Handy to know that, boy.' Fifteen minutes later, with Jesus Lopez tied down on the bay gelding, Cain was riding out with instructions from the boy on how to get to the Lazy R.

As he hit the trail Cain set his face into a stern mask. He did not have a notion what he was riding into, but whatever it was he would deal with it.

However, he held a deep curiosity as to why Wilson's Mexican wrangler should attempt to murder him. Dammit, he was just riding through. Why should anybody in this neck of the woods want to kill Jack Cain?

CHAPTER FIVE

It was almost nightfall when Cain entered the high but pleasant valley in which Wilson's Lazy R was situated. Climbing up the trail to it he noticed more farmhouses, surrounded by fences and ploughed fields with crops growing in them. He knew that, like a lot of legally claimed land these days, this range was most likely a powder keg waiting for somebody to light the blue paper. Cain also knew that cattlemen did not like sodbusters who settled on their territory. But the West was changing. Foreign immigrants and home-grown white Americans were buying up their 164 acres, taking advantage of the Homestead Act. However, that Act was proving to be a problem to those who settled this land. In the early days most cowmen didn't bother to register their holdings, thinking the ground they fought the Indians for, sweated over and died for, lynched the rustlers who were stealing their cows for, was theirs by God-given right. It was a severe shock to some to be told that things did not work that way any more, that compromises would have to be made. Agreements were being thrashed out; adjustments were being made but always providing that what was on offer was a reasonable settlement.

Cain stared ahead of him. The valley he was now riding down was maybe five miles long and a couple of miles across at its widest point. The rich grazing was belly-high to the roan. Making the ride even more enjoyable, a stream tinkled its way down the west side of the valley, clearly fed by streams from the distant mountains rising above the hills flanking the valley. As he took in the scenery he saw that mist, like will-o-the-wisps, was rising up from the river to spread like ghostly veils across the valley as the night cold crept in.

Cain shrugged deeper into his range coat. He lifted his gaze and ran it across the west lip of the valley and then the east. Considering he had already been shot at he figured it was a reasonable precaution to take. The east slope was still bathed in the last warm light of sunset. He noted that there was ample cover in the pines. Ambush country if ever he saw it. It was with a tense body and a hand on the Winchester in his saddle boot that he finished the rest of the journey.

The ranch house, he discovered, was at the head of the valley. It was a mud-caulked building made of pine logs topped by a sod roof. It was of similar construction to the Flying W dwelling, but smaller. There were three corrals. The largest one held ten mustangs. They were clearly unhappy at being penned in.

He turned his attention to the small bunkhouse close to the ranch and the ridge-roofed clapboard barn behind it. Two large sheds abutted the barn, one on each side. The whole place looked untidy but functional. However, unlike the Flying W, there were no flowers growing in front of this ranch, no curtains to the none-too-clean cheap glass in the windows. Even so, he could just see that there was a large, fenced vegetable plot at the rear of the building. It was packed with growing crops. It was a peaceful scene he looked at, made more so by the lazy column of blue-white wood smoke climbing up from the top of the yellow-stone chimney and into the ever-darkening sky. Sitting his mount before the building he called,

'The house?'

A tall, thin, fair-haired man came to the ranch house door. Out of the corner of his eye Cain also noticed two men appear at the bunkhouse door. One of them was holding a Winchester rifle, the barrel resting in the crook of his left arm, the right index finger laid along the trigger guard. It suggested that the Lazy R did not get many visitors and when they did they considered caution was needed.

Cain leaned over and undid the rope holding the body of Jesus Lopez on to the back of the well-behaved Flying W bay. He lifted one leg of the carcass and let the body drop to the worn ground. Then he stared at the man before him, framed in the ranch house doorway.

'You Matt Wilson?'

'Yes. What the hell is this?'

Cain pointed to the carcass. 'Believe he's one of yours.'

The Lazy R owner frowned and stepped down and came towards him. Cain noticed he was unarmed. When he reached him, Wilson stared at the body of Jesus Lopez for some moments before looking up with narrowed eyelids. 'Well, dammit, you'd better explain yourself, mister. Jesus Lopez was a top wrangler, a good man to have around. He'll be missed. Who shot him?'

'I did. He tried to ambush me.'

The lids across Wilson's pale blue eyes narrowed even further, until they were mere slits. 'Why, that's crazy,' he said. 'Ambush you? For why?'

Cain said, 'I was hoping you could tell me.'

Wilson stared, clearly puzzled. 'Why, I don't know you from Adam. And, dammit, how d'you know to bring him here?'

Cain explained the sequence of events that brought him here, watching Wilson closely while doing it. By the time he was finished Wilson's stare was round and held total incredulity.

'Jane Wilder's been shot, you say? Is she dead?'

'No, but she's awful sick.'

'And Lopez tried to pick you off?'

'Uh-huh.' Cain leaned forward in the saddle. 'Now I'm waiting for you to explain to me why he did.'

The Lazy R owner's stare became even more round. 'How the hell should I know?' He leaned forward. 'You don't think I sent Lopez?'

'It seems logical to me,' Cain said. 'You employed him.'

'Why, that's crazy,' Wilson said

The two range hands who had been standing in the bunkhouse doorway were now coming towards them. Cain saw that the 'puncher who was armed was still carrying his Winchester and he felt comforted by the fact that he had taken the precaution of unhooking the loop securing his Colt in its holster as he entered the valley. As the two came close the taller, carrying the Winchester, said, 'I heard what you were saying, mister, and you are talking shit. I rode with Lopez. He didn't strike me as being a bushwhacker.'

Cain leaned forward. 'Now listen to me, mister, I don't take kindly to be called a liar, implied or otherwise. As I have already explained to your boss, I've not been on this range more than half a day. In that time a woman has been shot and critically injured, a boy has been scared half out of his wits, and I have been used for target practice. Now, no matter how Lopez struck you, the hard fact of the matter is he tried his damnedest to kill *me*, and for that I want answers.'

The 'puncher stiffened and took a fresh grip on his rifle. 'Well, you won't get none here, mister. It doesn't make sense at all.'

Matt Wilson scrubbed his chin. Cain met his stare. 'Mister,' the Lazy R owner said, 'I had a loose arrangement with Lopez. He hired out all over the county and beyond when he wasn't needed here. Any one of a dozen on this range could have hired him.

Like Jim here, I never had Lopez down for a killer. All I can say is he must have been offered big money to do what he did.'

'Five hundred dollars' worth,' Cain said. 'It was in his pocket.'

Wilson shook his head. 'Well, he sure as hell did not get that kind of money from here. Right now, me and the boys are looking to make every saving we can, market being what it is at the moment.'

Cain now found he was at a loss what to think. Wilson and his men seemed genuine, and he did not base that opinion on whimsy. Having been a successful lawman for ten years he figured he could read men pretty good. He needed to if he was to survive in these lawless lands. However, on the other hand, he could get it wrong, and he had, big time, three months ago when Nate Creed's boy, Jacob, shot him down.

Not for the first time since it happened did that attempt on his life come back to Cain in all its vivid reality. The crack of the gun in the night, the searing pain in his chest as he spun and drew his Colt and fired in one fluid movement and killed the youth, even though he himself was going down badly wounded. The episode had left him deeply disillusioned, embittered. Simply because it turned out his attacker was the son of Nate Creed, the biggest rancher in Still County, a man he called friend for ten years and trusted implicitly. For long hours on his sickbed he puzzled over why Jacob had done such a thing until it came to light that the boy thought he was real slick with a gun and craved the notoriety he thought that ability would bring him if he shot down Sheriff Jack Cain, the renowned gunfighter and peace officer; the man who cleaned up Still County. Cain once again felt the deep sadness he'd endured on that day when he received the news. Dammit, he'd watched that boy grow up. He went riding with him, taught him to shoot; he had eaten Christmas dinner with him.

No one in the county blamed him for the killing except Nate Creed. In his misery, the rancher turned on his best friend, called him scum, a killer who needed hanging, and he would do his damnedest to see it done. But nobody in Still County would give that notion a second thought, despite Creed's influence over a wide area. There were too many witnesses to the cowardly ambush attempt made by his son. Every witness said Cain was left with no choice but to do what he did.

Cain looked now at the Lazy R owner and said, 'Wilson, one way and another I aim to get to the bottom of this. What's more, sure as hell, I don't like a woman being shot and left to die.'

The Lazy R owner stared. 'And you think I do?'

'I've got to keep an open mind on this, Wilson. Nobody's out of the frame until it's cleared up.'

The Lazy R owner said, with slight sarcasm, 'Spoken like a lawman.' Then he sighed and added, 'Have you ate yet, mister? I'd hate to deny a man range etiquette.'

Cain nodded his acceptance. 'Well, I got to say, that's decent of you, Wilson.' He looked down at

Lopez. 'Who gets to bury him?'

The rifle-holder, Jim, said, 'I'll bury him, soon as I've ate supper.' His companion added, 'Guess I'll help, too. Jesus rid with us for some time. Man needs some sort of burial, choose what he's done.'

'He'd rot there for me,' Cain said.

He dismounted tiredly and tethered his mount at the two-horse hitch rail before the ranch house. He followed Wilson into the house. The two hands came booting in behind. The room that Cain entered was comfortable, clean and functional, with mostly home-made furniture. A curtain in the far corner screened off a crude bed. Jim, the 'puncher with the Winchester, left the weapon leaning against the wall near the door.

Wilson led them through into the kitchen. A long, rough-hewn pinewood table to seat six was placed in the middle of the room. Cain saw that three hand-carved wooden bowls and spoons were laid out on it, and a platter was holding chunks of dark-brown bread. Two pine benches each side of the table took the place of chairs. The heat that met Cain as he entered the kitchen was like a slap in the face after the growing cool of the night outside.

An oven was in the far corner and the smell of meat-and-vegetable stew coming from the big cast-iron pan sitting on top of it was tantalizing.

Once they were all in Wilson turned to Cain and said, indicating the Winchester owner – a tall lean 'puncher with hawk features and staring brown eyes – 'This is Jim Struthers,' he said. Then he pointed to the short, bow-legged one with the puckish face and gimpy right leg. 'And this is Johnny Green.'

Cain nodded. 'Gents. Name's Jack Cain.'

Struthers' eyelids narrowed. 'Lawman over at Still County, am I right? Been a hell of a shindig over there so I heard, 'til you stamped on it. Heard you got shot near to death, though, in the end. Some rancher's son.'

'Well, he shot a bit straighter than Lopez, I got to say,' Cain said, 'but not straight enough. I survived and he didn't.'

Struthers said, 'You're a piece out of your way, mister.'

'I'm on my way to Montana, or was.'

Struthers shrugged as if he was indifferent to the information. He lifted a bowl from the table and went to the big stewpot. He filled the bowl to the brim with a thick mix of meat, potatoes and other vegetables. Green eagerly did likewise and with Struthers went to the table. Both sat down and ate hungrily. Meanwhile, Wilson went to the rough-hewn dresser set against the far wall and holding iron pans, wooden dishes and eating utensils. He came back carrying a bowl and spoon, which he handed to Cain.

'Just help yourself,' he said.

Cain did. Soon all were eating. For fully a minute they ate in silence. Then Wilson said, 'Cain, one time this range was peaceful, but I got to admit right now we have trouble, what with homesteaders moving in and all. But you know all about that, I guess, being a badge man down in Still County. However, there's a

59

twist to this one. Rumours are rife. Some say agents for wealthy Eastern business combines are operating in the area but I've seen no evidence of it. But whoever is doing it sure don't give a damn how they go about it.'

Cain said, 'How about Hanson? I know he wants to buy up the Flying W and has had big arguments with Frank Wilder about it, when Wilder was alive, that is.'

Wilson shook his head. 'I can't bring myself to believe it was Bart. Oh, I'll grant you he's aggressive and likes his own way on most things. And, yes, he's made no secret of the fact that he wants the Wilders' land. But I reckon he'll fall short of murder to gain that end. It just ain't his style.'

'How about you?' Cain said, 'you been approached?'

Wilson shook his head. 'Not so far; too small and too high, I guess. But, end of the day, who knows?'

'I passed farms along the way here,' Cain said.

Wilson shrugged. 'They've paid their dues on the land. They ain't bothered me none and I ain't bothered them.'

'Any other big ranchers?'

'Skeet Donavan, owns the Diamond D, over in the Big Paw hills. He settled the land along with Barton Hanson twenty years ago. He doesn't like what's going on. And, rumour is, he hasn't paid for an inch of that land he's sitting on and he's losing cattle to rustlers. He should get his ass into Eagle Rock and get matters sorted out.'

'How about Hanson?' Cain said. 'He owe?'

Wilson pursed his lips. 'Paid for most, as I under-
stand, and has got land grants on the rest. He owns
railroad stock. But that's Hanson's business, I guess.
I look to my own.' Wilson's look became enquiring.
'What you doing about tonight? There's a spare bed
in the bunkhouse if you want it.'

'That's real neighbourly of you, Wilson,' Cain said.
'Thanks.'

The Lazy R owner nodded. When the crocks were
washed up, they played cards until ten o'clock. Then
Struthers and Green went out to bury Lopez.

Cain slept the sleep of the just and woke up as the
dawn sun was pushing subdued rays through the one
stripped-hide window of the Lazy R bunkhouse. The
shards of light were hitting him full in the face.

He sat up, rubbed sleep out of his eyes, pushed his
blanket aside and lowered his stockinged feet to the
earth floor, eyeing the hole in the right stocking-toe
ruefully. He really would have to get it darned. A
quick glance told him that Jim Struthers' and Johnny
Green's bunks were empty. He had been so tired last
night, he did not hear the two come into the
bunkhouse after burying Lopez out on the range.

He got up pulled on his shirt, pants, vest, socks
and then his scuffed boots. At the pump in the yard
he washed the sleep out of his eyes and then he
walked to the ranch house, scattering the four dozen
or so hens and the rooster, which were pecking
around the worn open space. The cockerel eyed him
haughtily as he passed. The smell of fried bacon

permeating the air was pleasant to Cain's nostrils and it caused him to quicken his pace toward the ranch house.

Struthers and Green were coming out of the door as he approached. Wilson was behind them. They were all dressed ready for the range. It figured, because on the way over Cain noticed their horses saddled and tethered to the hitch rail. His own horse and the Flying W bay he had stabled in the barn last night, after playing cards. He fed them oats on Wilson's invitation. As he approached Wilson said, 'Got a big day today, Cain; more so now Lopez is out of the frame. Beans warming in the pan; help your-self to bacon and eggs.'

Cain nodded. Wilson's hospitality took him back to how it had been in the old days on the cow ranges. 'Thanks don't seem enough, Wilson.'

The Lazy R owner shrugged. 'Don't get many folk up here.' He squinted against the bright sun. 'Guess you'll be gone by the time we get back?'

'More than likely.'

All three were now astride their mounts and Wilson looked down on him from atop his grey horse. 'Maybe see you around, Cain?'

'It's a possibility.'

Struthers said, 'Still figuring on staying?'

'So far.'

The three then turned their mounts around and headed north into the green hills at a steady clip.

After watching them go Cain went into the kitchen and helped himself to beans and bacon. He took three eggs from a bowl holding at least a dozen and fried them in the bacon fat. He ate heartily, then pulled water from the pump over the sink and boiled water to wash up the crocks and shaved using Wilson's cut-throat razor and lather brush. He left them as he'd found them, stropped and clean. Half an hour later he was heading back to the Flying W.

He was eager to know about Jane Wilder and little Ethan before he went on into Eagle Rock to talk over the death of Jesus Lopez with Sheriff Maher. While he was about it he wanted to chew over with the lawman the general situation on this range. Maher must be the man to know, if he was doing his job properly.

Cain gazed at the beautiful day around him. Cotton wool clouds were floating across the big sky and the hill country was green and splendid. High mountains were white-topped in the far distance. It took little mental strain on Cain's part to decide this was God's own country.

He was moving out of the hills when he became aware of something hitting him with great force along the left side of his head. He could just vaguely hear the harsh crack of a rifle as he faded into deep darkness.

CHAPTER SIX

Cain became aware that a gnomelike man, dressed in greasy buckskins and slouch hat, was leaning over him. His bright, blue-grey stare was peering down at him out of a face that resembled a brown prune. Cain saw his hair was grey and long and it curled into the nape of his leathery neck. Cain reckoned the man could be no more than five foot four inches tall, but he was crouched and compact and every bit of him seemed to be sinewy muscle, as tough as rawhide. Cain also noted there was a big Bowie knife cased in a beaded sheath at his left hip. Regarding the man's age, Cain decided it was hard to tell. He could be sixty, but Cain got the distinct impression he was more like eighty though it appeared that ripe age was no handicap.

'If you ain't the luckiest of cusses,' the oldster was saying with a voice that resembled gravel rattling in a gourd.

'How so?' Cain said, trying to rise. The move caused terrific pain to punch like steel shafts into his skull and he winced.

The oldster giggled. 'That's how. Another inch to the right and you would have been crow bait, sonny.'

Cain groaned and pressed his hand to the left side of his head. All the demons in hell now seemed to be hitting him with sledgehammers. When he pulled his hand away he saw it was red with blood. It was then he recalled the sharp pain, the crack of a rifle before the deep blackness took him.

He focused on the oldster. 'Just who are you, mister?'

The oldster wrinkled a grin, revealing tobacco-blackened teeth. 'Me? I'm Medicine Bow Reynolds. You've heard of me. Ethan, down at the Flying W, mentioned me, didn't he?'

'He did.' Cain waved a hand weakly around him. 'You know what happened here, Reynolds?'

Medicine Bow cackled a laugh. 'You dumb or something? You got shot, that's what happened.'

Though resenting Medicine Bow's apparent relish for the situation, Cain said, 'Did you see who it was is what I'm asking?'

Medicine Bow shook his shaggy head. 'Naw. He was too far off. But I put a couple of shots his way. If I hadn't he would have finished you off for sure. I followed for a while but he was riding a real fast horse. Should have kept going, I guess, but I didn't know how bad you were. And seeing the boy has taken kindly to you I figured I'd best come back and see what, if anything, I could do.' The oldster shook his grizzled head. 'I don't like having unfinished

65

business on my hands, mister. I learned that fifty years ago in the Absarokas when them Blackfeet near took my scalp. I killed three of them but let one run, thinking I'd done enough to scare him off. Did I get that wrong! We fought near five minutes before I cut his gizzard out.'

Cain said, 'The wound, how bad is it?'

'You'll live but you'll have an awful big headache for a day or two.'

Cain slowly came to his feet, trying to ignore the fresh surge of pain the move caused, and waited for the waves of nausea to pass. Now he was standing he became aware that Medicine Bow was looking up at him. Cain could now see that he towered some eight inches above the oldster, but that did not detract from the impression Cain still got that mean power lay in this old man's wiry frame and that it could be turned on at the drop of a hat should the need arise.

He said, 'Well, I'll tell you what, Medicine Bow, I'm getting damned sick of people shooting at me.'

Reynolds cackled a laugh. 'Just be grateful the sons of bitches can't shoot straight, is all.' He screwed up his face in enquiry. 'D'you think you can ride?'

Cain said, 'There's only one way to find out. Where's the horses?'

'The bay headed off towards the Flying W,' Medicine Bow said, 'but I've git the roan tethered yonder.' He waved an arm to his rear, indicating a westerly direction. 'He didn't run far.'

'He's trained,' Cain said while following the old-timer's indication with searching grey eyes. In a clump of aspen and sycamore about fifty yards from where they were standing he saw his roan tied up alongside a wiry pinto mustang. The mustang must be Reynolds's horse. Cain now remembered Ethan telling him yesterday that Medicine Bow was down on the south range, mending wrecked fencing.

He said, 'Seeing how much you know, I take it you've been back to the ranch?'

'Rode in last night,' Reynolds said. 'Damned if I figured to find what I did, Jane shot up like that.' The oldster scratched his bristled chin. 'The boy told me about Lopez. You took him up to the Lazy R last night, right?'

'Yes.'

'What did Wilson say?'

'Said he didn't know why Lopez should be taking shots at me. In the end I came round to believing him.'

'Don't pay to trust people too much,' Medicine Bow said.

'I don't, usually,' Cain said.

Reynolds now wafted a hand to indicate the wound in Cain's skull. 'Seems you've got more lives than a damned cat, surviving this one. Let me tell you, boy, if you'd been in Blackfeet country in the old days you'd have been long dead by now, riding around so unprepared.'

'Well, we're not in Blackfeet country,' Cain said, a little tetchy at being accused of such carelessness.

'Jest thank God ye ain't,' Reynolds said. He crinkled up his eyelids like he was squinting against a strong sun. 'So, what d'you aim to do now?'

'Ride to the Flying W, to see if everything is all right.'

'It's all right,' Medicine Bow said. 'Lodge Woman is looking after things, but won't do any harm for one of us to stay close, I guess.'

Cain began walking towards his horse. He tried to ignore the pain and dizziness that was still assailing him. Medicine Bow fell in beside him, rolling like a seaman on his short bow legs. As they walked Cain said, 'What are you doing out here, Medicine Bow? Though, to be sure, don't think I'm not grateful for it.'

'Looking for any sign the bastard that shot Jane left.'

'You had any luck?'

Medicine Bow made a sour face. 'Nary a crumb; maybe I'm getting old.'

When they reached the horses Cain climbed into the saddle. He made for his handkerchief in his pants pocket, pulled it out and held it to his skull. Then he said, looking down at the old man, 'Just where do you fit into this, old-timer? You kin to the Wilders, or something?'

Reynolds spat a stream of tobacco juice to the grass. 'Well, that's easy to explain, though I ain't kin as such,' he said. 'See, I was friendly with Jane's grandpappy in the beaver days. When he decided to settle I kept in touch with him and Dora, his wife, and subsequently their issue and the issue of that issue. Ain't seen Frank and Jane and the boys for some time so six weeks ago I happened to be passing through on my way to Cheyenne and decided to call. Soon as I saw how things were with Jane and the boy, family dead and all and being rustled near out of house and home, I felt I'd be a real mean critter not to stay on and see what I could do to help.'

Cain said, 'That's what friends are for, I guess.'

'It goes deeper than that, boy, way deeper,' Medicine Bow said. 'Back in the old days Jane's grandpappy pulled me out of one hell of a fix with the Sioux. I was grateful to him – life's precious – and I will be grateful to him through his kin for the rest of my life.' He waved a brisk right hand. 'Now, go and git your damned fool head fixed. Lodge Woman is mighty good at such things.' The mountain man's gaze turned inquisitive. 'By the way, are you staying on at the Flying W?'

'I don't like being shot at,' Cain said. He placed his hands on the saddle horn and leaned forward. 'And, d'you know something, Medicine Bow? I got a feeling the bastard that shot Mrs Wilder was the same galoot that took a shot at me just now. Where Jesus Lopez fits into this equation I haven't figured out yet – he's a wild card – but I sure as hell aim to find out.'

'Well, I like optimism,' Reynolds said. He screwed up his eyelids in enquiry once more. 'You a lawman one time?'

'Yes.'

'Guess that explains your cussedness.'

Cain tried a smile, though it hurt, and turned his

horse. 'Maybe it does. I'll be seeing you, Medicine Bow.'

Reynolds's warning followed him. 'Keep your eyes peeled, Cain. I've got a feeling that son of a bitch is still around.'

'You've got that feeling, too, huh?' Cain said.

'Yeah, so heed it.'

Cain eased the Winchester in his saddle boot and the Colt in his holster and said, 'Will do,' and headed to the Flying W.

CHAPTER SEVEN

But nobody took any further shots at Cain and two hours later he climbed down before the Flying W hitching rail and tethered the roan next to a strange horse that was also tied up there. He saw that the bay he had used to take Lopez to the Lazy R was back in the corral, chewing on the hay-bale hanging over the rails.

He was walking up the path holding a head that was still throbbing fit to burst when a short, powerful-looking man came to the door and blocked his way. He was wearing a grey pinstripe suit, black string tie and brown Stetson. Trousers were tucked into brown high boots. There was a Colt Sheriff nestled in the holster at the man's right thigh. Cain also noticed a star showing through the gap of his open jacket. It was pinned to his blue shirt.

'Jack Cain?' the lawman said.

'You've found me. You Sheriff Neal Maher?'

'Yes.'

Cain motioned with a hand. 'Well, I need to get

my head fixed right now, Maher. We can talk while it's being done.'

The sheriff remained, blocking the doorway. 'I want you to come into Eagle Rock with me, right now.'

Cain frowned. 'What's the rush and what the hell for?'

'You know what for,' Maher said. 'The killing of Jesus Lopez. Lopez was a popular figure on this range.'

'Popular?' Cain glared his disgust. 'Maher, the bastard tried to kill me; pumped eight shots in my direction. Not only that, I was shot at on my way here from the Lazy R. Another inch to the right and I would have been dead meat. What are you going to do about that, now that you know?' Cain leaned forward until he was but two inches from the face of the serious-looking sheriff of Eagle Rock. He added, 'Mister, if you haven't noticed, you don't exactly have a law-abiding range here. And while we're on the subject of killing, what are you doing about catching Mrs Wilder's husband's killer, her boy Brian's killer and the two range hands that were shot . . . not to mention the rustling going on?' He squinted. 'And what about Mrs Wilder's shooting?' He waved a hand toward the bedrooms. 'She's lying near to death in there.'

The colour in Maher's bland face heightened. 'I do the best I can with the tools I've got.'

'If you ask me, you ain't doing enough.'

Cain pushed brusquely past Maher and into the

big common room. He found it was empty. He was expecting to see Ethan and Lodge Woman sitting here. He had figured that Maher would have herded them in here to keep an eye on them.

He turned to go into the kitchen but the bore of Maher's Colt Sheriff jabbed into his ribs. Cold anger seeped through Cain. He levelled his now icy gaze on to the Eagle Rock lawman. He said, 'Put the gun away, Maher. It isn't me you want. Now, where's the boy?'

Maher said, 'In the barn.'

'Lodge Woman?'

'In the kitchen, but you've no need to be bothered about them.'

'You reckon?'

Once more Cain attempted to push past Maher. The lawman jabbed the Colt Sheriff harder into his ribs. He said, 'You're not understanding me, Cain, I want you in for questioning.'

Quick as lightning Cain grabbed and twisted the four-inch barrelled Colt out of Maher's hand and threw it across the big room. It clattered metallically against the far wall. Already cocked, it exploded and lead embedded itself into the far log wall with a soapy *thunk*.

Cain said, crisply, 'Now, get the hell out of my way, mister, for I'm through playing games.'

Just then Lodge Woman came hurrying into the room. 'Who shoot?' she said. Then she saw the wound on the side of Cain's head. 'You hit, Cain? I fix. Me heap good medicine woman.'

'That is what I am hoping for.'

Ethan came running into the room now, from outside. He stared at Cain. 'What happened, sir?'

Cain patted him on the shoulder. 'Nothing to worry about, boy,' he said. 'The sheriff dropped his Colt. He's just leaving.' Cain stared at the Eagle Rock lawman. 'Ain't that right, Maher?'

Maher, clearly livid, said, 'I came here peaceful, Cain.'

'I'm not stopping you leaving the same way,' Cain said. 'But to keep your daybook tidy, Maher, Lopez shot at me from the cover of that butte yonder. He must have let off at least eight shots before I managed to nail him. The evidence is up there, in the hulls he left behind, if you care to look.' Cain dabbed his wound gently. 'Now, further to that, what d'you aim to do about the son of a bitch that nearly put my lights out on the range just now?'

Maher said, briskly, 'It'll be looked into.'

'Like you looked into Frank Wilder's killing and the others?'

Maher's cheeks turned bright red this time. 'I told you, my resources are limited!'

'Too limited if you ask me.'

After a long stare, in which he appeared to be weighing up the situation, the Eagle Rock lawman paced across the room. He picked up his Colt, holstered it, turned and stalked out, glaring at Cain as he went. Soon the sound of hoofbeats came. Then Cain realized that Lodge Woman was pushing him towards the kitchen.

'You want head fixing?' she said. 'You got headache?'

'Headache ain't the word, Lodge Woman,' Cain said tiredly.

The Crow woman frowned as if puzzled. 'What is name, then?'

'It *is* the word, all right.' Cain grinned at her as best he could. 'Just making silly white talk, I guess.'

Lodge Woman glared. 'You no make silly white talk with me, mister, if you do I no fix head, huh?'

Cain nodded. 'Fair enough.'

'Sure fair enough,' said the Crow woman.

She bustled him into the kitchen. Soon his head was cleaned of both wet and dried blood, treated with some preparation and bandaged. After that she gave him an oral concoction – for 'bad head', she said. It tasted foul but Cain downed it and then sat there in the kitchen trying to come to terms with all that was going on; trying to figure what to do about it.

Medicine Bow was out after the ambusher. Cain was confident the old-timer was more than capable of taking care of that side of things, if the stories about mountain men were true. As for Ethan . . . the boy must still be hurting after his recent experiences. One way to fix that, to Cain's knowledge anyway, was to take the boy's mind off things. He remembered now that some shingles above the gallery needed fixing. He looked at the boy, who was standing in the kitchen doorway gazing at him. 'How's your mother, son?'

Before the boy could answer Lodge Woman said, 'She doing fine, Cain; you ask me when want to know about Jane Wilder, huh? Boy not medicine woman. Me medicine woman; boy is boy.'

Cain tried to look grave. 'I stand corrected.'

'Huh.'

Cain looked at Ethan. He said, 'I saw some shingles needed fixing over the gallery just now, boy. How about you and me getting the job done?'

Ethan's face lit up immediately. 'I know where all Pa's tools are, sir,' he said. 'And there are shingles cut out the back. Medicine Bow and me made them last week, but we never got round to fixing them. We've been fence-mending near the Coyote Ridge line camp most of the week.'

'Medicine Bow's been keeping you busy, huh, boy?'

'Yes, sir; said it would be good for me.'

Cain nodded his approval. 'He said right. Well, let's get to it.'

An hour and a half an hour later three riders came in from the hills and dusted into the worn space beyond the front garden. Coming up behind was a flatbed wagon. Slowing his pace along with the other riders, the flatbed driver eased the chestnut in the shafts to a stop. Then a tall, lean man, with a face that was tanned to deep brown eased his big grey forward until its muzzle was almost touching the wicket gate. Cain noticed that the fellow wore a Colt, holstered high on his right hip. It was not a gunslinger's rig.

76

Cain stared down at him from his position on the roof and moved the hammer he was using into his left hand, freeing up his right one, which he moved nearer to his own belt weapon.

Ethan said, quietly, 'It is King Laker, sir, owns the Floating L. Medium-size outfit by Bear Paw Creek fifteen miles north-west.'

Cain said, 'Thanks, boy.'

'You Cain?' Laker said. His voice was harsh and dry.

'That's right,' Cain said. 'What can I do for you, Laker?'

The Floating L owner frowned. 'How d'you know my name?'

'The boy told it. What's this about?'

'Killing Jesus Lopez is what it is about.' His words were backed up by the metallic clicks of Winchesters being armed and Cain raised his gaze to see the three men behind Laker and the man on the cart were levelling up their rifles.

Cain turned his stare on to Laker. It was not friendly. 'Just what the hell is this, mister? That son of a Mexican bitch asked for all he got.'

'We don't know that,' Laker said. 'Lopez was no bushwhacker.'

'The hell he wasn't,' Cain said. 'You got his pedigree, or something?'

'No, I ain't, but—'

As slick as quicksilver, Cain palmed his Colt and levelled it at Laker's forehead, arm out straight. He looked down and, momentarily, he allowed his gaze to run along the lined-up men before him. Then he focused on the Floating L owner once more. 'Get this through your head, Laker,' he said quietly. 'I take exception to men pointing guns at me. Worse, putting children's lives at risk while doing it. Now, tell your men to put up their weapons so we can talk like reasonable men.'

Laker stared for some moments. After a couple of seconds of gazing into the big bore of Cain's Colt he said, 'OK, men, easy now.'

Winchesters were lowered reluctantly and hammers were taken off the armed position, causing a disorganized rattle of metal clicks to disturb the still, hot air. Satisfied, Cain now flicked a glance in Ethan's direction. 'Move on into the house, boy, while I take care of this.'

'I want to stay with you,' Ethan said.

'Don't argue with me, son, just do it.'

Mumbling his protests Ethan climbed down the ladder and went into the house. Cain now allowed his icy gaze to seize fully the owner of the Floating L's grey stare. He said, 'Now we've got an understanding, Laker, what's Lopez to you?'

'A damn fine horse-breaker, that's what.'

'Well, he ain't any more.'

Laker said, 'You made damn sure of that.'

'Bet your boots I did,' Cain said. 'Señor Lopez put eight shots my way before I got the chance to nail him. But don't take my word for it. The evidence is on the bluff up there, if you care to take a look.'

Laker shook his head fervently, apparently only

half-convinced by Cain's words. 'It ain't like him,' he protested. 'Dammit, it ain't.'

'So I keep being told, but it happened nonethe-less.'

Ethan called from the doorway, 'I been up there, too, with Medicine Bow Reynolds. Medicine Bow says Mr Cain is telling the truth.'

Laker flicked a glance at the boy in the doorway and suddenly he looked unsure of his ground. 'Well, I respect Medicine Bow's opinion,' he said. 'Even so . . . it still don't make a deal of sense.'

Cain said, 'Take some advice, Laker, and leave this to me. I'll get to the bottom of it.'

'I've read about you, Cain,' the Floating L owner said. 'Lawman, right? Broke the back of that range war they had down Still County recently.'

'I'm finished with all of that,' Cain said.

'If you is,' Laker said, 'then you're contradicting yourself.'

Cain set his chin. 'It's unfinished business. I don't like being shot at and I don't like women being half-shot to death either.'

Laker said resentfully, 'You figure *I* do?' He moved uneasily in the saddle and then made a conciliatory gesture with his right hand. 'Speaking of Mrs Wilder, how is she? I heard she's been shot bad. Fact is, I came to see if I could do anything, but when I saw you here—'

'You went off half cocked,' Cain said.

Laker glared. 'I had to find out, dammit!'

'Maybe,' Cain said. 'Well, Mrs Wilder is recovering, but she ain't out of the woods yet.'

Laker seemed relieved by that and said, 'Something, I guess.' The Floating L owner now seemed at a loss as to what to say next. He fiddled with the reins for a moment before he turned to his men and said, 'Well, I guess we're through here, boys. Let's ride.'

But Cain wasn't through. He held up a hand, his face grim. He said, 'Hold it right there, Laker. You made a big show of caring for Lopez's hide just now. Seeing as you were so cosy with that Mexican son of a bitch, was it you who sent him to kill me?'

Laker's stare was full of incredulity. 'Are you crazy? I don't even know you.'

Cain said, 'Well, somebody sure sent him.' He continued to stare at the Floating L owner before he added, 'Just what in the hell is going on, on this range, Laker? You got any ideas on that?'

Laker shrugged, as if ignorant. 'You tell me. It's been going on about six months now. Most blame Eastern speculators, but I ain't so sure.'

'Why, have you been bothered?'

'I lost one hundred head only the other week,' Laker said. 'Two hundred a month ago. One hand was killed in that. Mister, I'm only a small outfit, I can't take those kinds of losses for long.'

'Did you find out who did it?'

'Naw. They got clean away.'

'What did Sheriff Maher do?'

'Organized a posse. My three men and I joined it. We were out for a week, but nothing came of it.'

'Could it be nesters?' Cain said.

Laker shook his head. 'Naw, it isn't nesters. Oh, they've been known to take the odd steer or two to keep the wolf from the door, but not the losses I've been taking.'

Cain said, 'How d'you feel about nesters moving in?'

'Well, I'm not overpowered with goodwill, if that's what you mean,' Laker said. 'But they've bought their land, like me, so I guess they have title to it.'

'You say you've bought your land? You're not on free range?'

Laker shook his head. 'No, I read the signs after hearing about what was happening in other ranges. The West's growing up, mister. The law is arriving and there isn't free range any more. So I filed on all the prime land I have, and now I protect my own.'

'Wise man,' Cain said.

The Floating L owner gave him a serious look. 'I think so. Now, you've been asking all the questions, how about me asking you one: what are your plans, Cain, if you're not moving on?'

'Haven't decided. I'm making it up as I go along,' Cain said. He squinted. 'What's your view on why the Wilders have been hit so hard?'

Laker shook his head. 'I don't know, apart from the Flying W has some of the best grazing on the whole damn range.' He sighed. 'Well, guess we'd best ride now. Supposed to be picking up supplies in Eagle Rock. Jest made a detour to find out if I could do anything for Jane.'

81

Cain said, 'Good for you. Been interesting talking to you, Laker.'

Laker nodded, narrowed his eyelids. He said, 'Guess I had you figured wrong, Cain, but I'm not about to apologize. However, I'd be interested to know why Lopez took those shots at you. If you ever git to finding out, let me know.'

The Floating L bunch was topping the rise in the trail to Eagle Rock when Sheriff Maher passed them on the brow. Behind Maher rode four men. Their outlines were familiar. Slow anger filled Cain. From what he knew so far he was not of the opinion that Maher was wearing the badge that Cain held in such respect with any kind of honour. Now, seeing the men he was riding with at this moment confirmed that opinion.

Cain climbed down the ladder from the roof and stood waiting on the garden path for Maher's posse to arrive.

He loosened the Colt in its holster.

CHAPTER EIGHT

At that moment Ethan joined him. The boy was carrying the shotgun. Cain said, 'You intending to use that, boy?'

'If I have to. I have been meaning to since you sent me inside.'

'You mean you had Laker covered?'

'Yes, sir,' Ethan said, 'but I wouldn't have shot unless he drew his Colt. Even then I would have gone for the riders behind him. I figured you would have been taking care of Mr Laker yourself.'

Cain stared at the button. Ethan's stature was growing by the hour, but the boy must learn restraint; learn that violence, in the end, counts for nothing unless it is for the good. He had learned long ago that, at the end of the day, no matter what, men must finally sit down and talk out their differences. Unfortunately, they seldom did until too much blood had been spilt and too many lives had been lost.

He said, 'Boy, you've got to be sure about your shooting afore you do it. If you do it rashly and hit the wrong fellow, then there's usually no way back for him and a life has been wasted.'

'So Pa said.'

Cain said, 'He did, huh? Seems to me he was quite a man, your pa.'

'I miss him real bad, sir.'

Cain felt another tender moment for the boy. There had never been too many kind moments in his life. When there were they usually embarrassed him immensely. In the end he found the best way to deal with them was to avoid getting too involved.

Nevertheless, with an instinctive gesture he rested his hand on Ethan's blond locks and said, 'I'm sure you do, boy, but it'll pass. All things do in the end, though you may not believe it now.'

Sheriff Maher was now up to the gate, but Cain's main interest was the four men lined up with the lawman. Jed Stinger, Bud Allen, Freddie Knot and George Powell. He knew them to be hardcases to a man. He'd run them out of Still County. He turned his gaze on to the sheriff. 'I thought we'd settled this, Maher.'

'You don't know me very well, Cain.' Maher waved a hand. 'Boys, explain to the ex-lawman my philosophy.'

Slick as China silk four guns were drawn and Cain found he was effectively covered by a variety of hand-weapons. From long experience he knew that to try something now would mean that both he and the boy would be gunned down without qualm, for the men flanking Neal Maher knew no pity. They just took the big dollar for their services until it was their turn to die.

Ethan was bringing up the shotgun. Cain pushed it down. 'Don't be a damned fool, boy,' he said quietly. 'These men play for keeps. Put the weapon on the ground and do it now.'

'But—'

'Just do it, son.'

Stinger leaned forward, a grin on his face and spat juice. 'Spunky kid you got there, Cain,' he said.

Cain ignored the hardcase and turned to Maher. 'What now?'

'Shuck your handgun,' Maher said. 'I'm taking you in.'

Cain threw down his Colt. 'You need killers to do your dirty work now, Maher?'

'They are legally sworn-in deputies.'

'I know them all, Maher,' Cain said. 'I chased them all out of Still County when the game was up.'

'Chased hell,' Jed Stinger said. He leaned his big frame forward again and stared with eyes that were as cold and blue as Arctic ice. 'Just weren't the money in it any more. We got a better offer.'

Cain stared. 'So do tell. I'd be interested.'

George Powell said, 'Shut it, Stinger.'

Stinger sniggered. 'Well, you're right. It don't do for a man to know too much about our business, now do it? Even if he is walking dead.'

Maher said, 'Get your horse, Cain.' He turned to

Bud Allen. 'Follow him into the barn, Bud, see he doesn't do anything stupid.'

'Sure will do that, Sheriff.'

Allen was a tall, lean, narrow-faced man with a dark moustache, the ends of which curled under the bottom of his cleft chin. He permanently wore a half-smile, though it was never one inspired by humour: it was more of a sneer. The scar Cain had given him a year ago with a bullet from a Colt .45 was now a livid mark across the right side of his face.

Allen was still grinning as he eased his big chestnut mare forward. With brutal suddenness he slashed down with the Smith & Wesson American in his hand. Cain stood, momentarily stunned, after the barrel cut across his face. The blow enhanced the pain he was already suffering due to the bullet crease in his skull. He felt blood tricking warmly down his face. Cold anger filled him.

'Reckon we're quits now, you bastard,' Allen said, his stare evil. 'Now get to doing what Maher wants.'

Cain began to reach for his handkerchief in his shirt pocket but Allen waved the Smith & Wesson aggressively. 'Like hell you do.'

Cain glared his wrath. 'I want something to stop the bleeding, dammit.'

'Too bad for you. Move.'

Cain turned to the boy, who he saw was made wide-eyed and open mouthed by the sudden violence. 'Go in to Lodge Woman, Ethan.'

'I want to stay with you!'

Lodge Woman appeared in the doorway and stepped down the path. She gave Cain a piece of cloth to use on the wound. Then turned to the boy and grabbed him by the collar. 'Do as Cain says.'

Cain looked at her. 'Look after him 'til I get back, Lodge Woman.'

'I look after Jane Wilder's boy, anyhow.'

George Powell guffawed. 'You think you're coming back, Jack? We got unfinished business, you and me, always providing you avoid the hang rope, of course. Killing that poor innocent greaser like that. Pheew! What a thing to do.'

Unfinished business. Cain set his jaw into a determined line. Yeah, we've got that all right. Six months ago he'd put Powell in bed for a week with a wound to his shoulder. The old regret came back. He should have killed the murderous bastard when he had the chance.

He turned and stared at Maher. 'Is this your idea of law enforcement?'

Maher said, 'Just go get your horse, Cain. You should have come peaceable the first time.'

'I haven't done nothing wrong!'

'That is for the jury to decide.'

After glowering at Maher, Cain walked toward the first barn. Bud Allen followed on behind leading his pinto, his Smith & Wesson American trained on Cain's spine. In the barn Cain went to the stall holding his roan and saddled up. Now mounted, he walked his roan over to Maher. Behind him, Allen eased up into his saddle, while keeping his gun trained on the middle of Cain's broad shoulders. As he reached Maher, Cain found one question burning in his brain.

'Will I get to Eagle Rock alive?'

Maher stared. He said, 'What do you think this is, Cain? A vigilante party? You'll get a fair trial.'

Cain curled his lips into a sneer. 'If that jury is true, Maher, then this is a waste of your time and mine. Lopez asked for all he got. I was defending myself, simple as that. Like I told you, the evidence is up there.'

'So you keep saying.'

Stinger jeered, 'You're a damned killer, Cain, like the rest of us, and don't pretend you ain't.'

Ignoring him, Cain looked at Ethan, who was standing in the doorway. He said, 'I'll be back, son, you see.'

'The hell you will,' Bud Allen said. 'Your goose is cooked.'

The lean hardcase dismounted, picked up Cain's rifle, which was lying in the dust, and smashed it against the nearest cottonwood. Then he emptied Cain's Colt of bullets, slid out the cylinder and threw it to hell and gone before casting the rest of the weapon aside. Next, he ejected the shells in Ethan's shotgun before breaking it against a tree. Then he stared at Ethan menacingly. 'Just in case you get the wrong idea, boy, and we have to come back and kill you.'

Laughter filled the air from the hardcases: cold, harsh laughter that caused a feeling similar to ice

water to start trickling down Cain's spine.
This was not a good situation.

CHAPTER NINE

Cain's head was aching fit to bust and the jog of the horse on the ride into Eagle Rock did him no favours. He entered town not in the best of humours. More so, because of the bunch of killers surrounding him.

Cain found Eagle Rock was big for a cow town. He deduced the reason for that must be down to the railroad branch line that came out of the shimmering flat plain to his right. Affirming his deduction, to his right they passed huge cattle-pens and sidings. It suggested that all the steers on this range were trailed to here before being shipped out to the meat-processing factories in Chicago and other large Eastern cities. From that he confidently assumed that big money changed hands here. And to satisfy the needs of the boys who drove those steers and were looking for some relaxation after hard days on the trai, he noticed that there were four saloons, two dancehalls, a theatre and a gaudy, red-painted whorehouse half a mile up the north trail out of town.

Judging from the prosperous look to the place, Cain decided there must also be a brisk trade in food supplies, as well as hay, grain and equipment of all kinds pertaining to the ranchers and the farmers who were settling this range. It also seemed that, due to the bad winters they got in this high country, most of the buildings were substantial. That suggested that Eagle Rock must have existed for quite some time and was built to make living bearable through the worst of the winter months.

Arriving at the yellow-stone sheriff's office, with the jailhouse at the rear, Maher said, 'Climb down, Cain.'

Cain stiffly complied. Maher now nodded to the men flanking him. 'OK, boys, I'll take it from here.'

'As you say,' George Powell said. He grinned at the other hardcases. 'Guess drinks are in order, huh, boys . . . maybe some cards?'

'Been a thirsty ride for sure and I do feel lucky,' Bud Allen said, matching Powell's leer.

Cain now met Powell's cold, mocking stare when it turned on to him. 'Hope to be seeing you soon, Jack, in case that jury gets it wrong.'

Cain's stare resembled two pieces of flint. 'I should have finished the job on you first time.'

Powell continued to grin. 'But you didn't, Jack, and that was your mistake.'

With the rest of the hardcases Powell eased his mount around and headed for Jason's Saloon and

Diner, almost opposite to the law office. At the ten-horse tie rail fronting it the four dismounted and entered.

Maher gestured with his Colt. 'Inside, Cain.'

'Pleasant company you keep, Maher,' Cain said with heavy sarcasm. He mounted the boardwalk and crossed to the law office.

'They do the job,' Maher said.

'What kind of council sanctions such scum as that to keep the peace?'

'I sometimes wonder myself,' Maher said.

That odd remark brought Cain to an abrupt halt. 'That's strange talk, coming from you.'

'You reckon?' Maher waved the Colt again. 'Inside.'

But Cain waited, hoping for more. When he didn't get it he moved into the law office.

He found the interior functional: two chairs, one a swivel, a gun rack containing three Winchester rifles. A Greener shotgun was sitting on two dowel pegs hammered into the far wall. A big desk with papers strewn on it was situated not far from the rifle rack. As they entered a hawk-faced deputy eased himself out of the swivel-chair behind the desk and said, 'You got him, then.'

'Open up cell one and put him in, Clem,' Maher said.

Deputy Clem Frazer plucked keys off a hook also set into the far wall, waved a hand at Cain and said, 'Head for that door, mister.'

The open door the deputy indicated was substantial. Cain moved reluctantly towards it while staring at the sheriff of Eagle Rock. He said, 'You're making a big mistake here, Maher. I'm not the man you should be locking up.'

Maher frowned. 'Oh! Who is it, then?'

'Dammit, that's for you to find out,' Cain said. 'You haven't been trying too hard by all accounts.'

'Don't believe all you hear, Cain.'

Clem Frazer poked him in the back with the Colt now in his hand. 'First cell you come to, fellow.'

Cain walked through the door. To the right was a wall of bars, separated into three cells with more bars. In each were uncomfortable-looking bunks and a slop bucket. None of the cells was occupied.

Cain walked through the first open cell door. He turned as the door clanged to behind him, gripped the bars and stared into Frazer's grey eyes as the deputy locked him in. But Frazer ignored the look. Now Cain saw that Maher was standing in the frame of the door separating the cellblock from the office. The sheriff stepped back to allow his deputy to pass him, then stood there as if he was considering something.

'Is there a date for the hearing, seeing as you are so eager?' Cain said.

'Noon tomorrow. Judge Collins is already in town.'

'This is a hell of a thing, Maher,' Cain said, 'and you know it.'

'No man likes to be behind bars,' Maher said.

'I don't mean that. Who wants me dead?'

Maher stared but said nothing.

'This whole thing stinks to high heaven,' Cain said. 'Are you pretending you don't know that?'

Maher found his voice. 'You'll get a fair trial.'

Cain said, 'Like hell I will. Something fishy is going on here and you are a damned fool if you don't know it.'

Maher took a swift glance back into the office. Then he whispered; 'I'll talk to you later. This ain't the time'

Cain stared. '*What?*'

But before he could demand of Maher what he meant the sheriff of Eagle Rock turned and closed the door behind him. Cain stared through the bars at the stout boards while trying to come to terms with his frustration as well as attempting to cope with his pain.

His head was thumping like the beating of a drum and the blow to the face he'd taken from Bud Allen's Smith & Wesson wasn't helping matters. He sat down heavily on the hard bunk and held his head in his hands. Christ, what was he doing here? What was happening to him? He was just passing through this damned country, for God's sake!

He eased back and lay supine on the bunk, his hands clasped behind his bandaged head. He stared at the flyspecked ceiling. He tried to make sense of all that was occurring, but couldn't because it didn't make any sense. Dammit, mid-morning yesterday he was happily heading for Montana, looking forward to a new life and not remotely interested in other people's troubles any more. He'd resolved many weeks ago, on his sick bed, he was through with all of that.

More waves of nausea hit him. He waited for the mists to clear and the pain to ease. He needed to think straight. He closed his eyes. Sleep would come, he knew, for, no matter what the circumstances, he had trained himself to catch up on his sleep when and where he could. In this land of the lawless, and especially with him being a police officer, there was often little opportunity for sleep when trouble reached high noon.

Slumber soon enveloped him despite his hurts.

CHAPTER TEN

The door to the cells opened, waking Cain. He sat up, the remnants of sleep clearing fast. But his head still thumped like a stamp mill. He carefully felt at Lodge Woman's bandages. They were still in place. Neal Maher now came into the cell area carrying a tray of food. At the bars the sheriff bent and passed it under the three-inch gap at the bottom.

'How are you feeling?' he said, as if he cared.

Cain picked up the tray. On it was a bowl of stew and a mug of oily-looking coffee. He prepared to eat but before he did he said, his stare like two edges of steel blades, 'Are you some kind of hypocrite? Where's your gorillas? Sent them home?'

'They're only used when needed.'

'Used for what? Killing?'

Maher just stared in that blank way he had, so Cain decided to try and jolt him out of his complacency. 'You still ain't told me who is pulling your strings.'

As if he would.

Maher opened his mouth as if to make a swift

retort but held it and leaned close to the cell bars. His voice came as a whisper once more. 'Listen good, Cain. Come midnight you'll be getting out of here.'

Cain stared his disbelief, the first spoonful of stew poised between mouth and plate and temporarily forgotten. He said, 'What the hell are you talking about?'

'There'll be your horse and guns waiting,' Maher went on. 'The plan I'll explain later.'

'Plan? What damned plan?' But Maher was already on his way out of the cellblock, the separating door closing with a hollow clunk behind him.

Cain stared at the stout oak boards once more as he lifted the forkful of stew the rest of the way to his mouth. He chewed. The meat was as tough as boot leather and he quickly suspected it was horse, sent to the knacker's yard because it was worked out and of no further use.

As he chewed deep suspicion filled him. Was lapdog Maher planning to get Cain, the increasingly troublesome ex-sheriff of Still County, who had unwittingly got involved in this chilling situation of blood-letting and plundering, out of the way so that that process could continue? Was it Maher's intention to trap ex-sheriff Cain? He could see the headlines in the local rag now:

EX-LAWMAN TURNED BAD. SHOT DEAD WHILE TRYING TO ESCAPE THE JUSTICE HE SO RICHLY DESERVED FOR GUNNING DOWN JESUS LOPEZ WHO, AS WE ALL

KNOW, WAS A POPULAR AND VALUABLE
MEMBER OF OUR RANGE COMMUNITY.

Cain shook his head. No, he was thinking crazy.
But then, this was the craziest of situations. He
spooned in another mouthful of stew and chewed on
it. He was fast coming to the conclusion that Maher
was in cahoots with whoever it was that was stirring
up trouble on this range. Everything was pointing
that way. And it wasn't just fanciful thinking. Cain
knew of other lawmen who had cashed in on a situation like this when the money offered to turn a blind
eye was too attractive to refuse. Was Maher one of
those?

Cain found his body tightening up. The prospect
of having to face up to yet another attempted
ambush was a daunting one, though he was ready to
do that if it meant getting out of here so he could get
to grips with what was going on. For, sure as hell, that
was what he avidly wanted to do now. Or was he
letting his imagination run away with him and Maher
had some genuine proposition?

He finished the rest of his meal and coffee, then
lay back on the bunk and waited for Maher's next
move. Meanwhile, the sun set, its last rays etching the
shadows of the window bars in the square of light it
cast on the whitewashed wall opposite. As was usual,
twilight lingered before full dark set in. An out-of-
tune piano now struck up a lively melody, deep in the
heart of town.

Again Cain clamped his throbbing, bandaged

head in his hands and rested his elbows on his knees. It wasn't long before he stretched out on the bunk once more and stared at the stars in a sky of dark-purple velvet, framed in the small square of the barred cell window. He listened to a dog barking in town, the female voice bawling at it to shut up. Half an hour later a coyote yipped, way out on the dark range. Then a chorus of them began yapping. It was a lonely, eerie, primeval sound.

The hours dragged by. It got so late Cain began to think Maher's terse offer of horse and guns was just a cruel joke, born out of his twisted, scheming mind. He tried to get comfortable. Then, maybe half an hour later, he heard the soft buzz of voices, which had been coming from the office beyond the cell door most of the evening, end in the louder call of, 'Well, see you tomorrow, Neal.'

'Six o'clock prompt, Clem.'

'Have I ever let you down?'

'Guess not.'

A door closed.

Fully alert, Cain came up on his elbow. Five minutes later the door to the cellblock opened and Maher walked in.

Cain uncoiled off the bunk, crossed to the cell bars and gripped them. His stare met the Eagle Rock sheriff's bland gaze. 'OK,' he said, 'you were talking about guns and horses.'

'I want you on the outside, Cain.'

The old suspicions resurrected themselves in Cain's mind. He said, 'So you can gun me down like a dog soon as I leave the office and then proclaim to the gullible public of Eagle Rock what a great and vigilant lawman you are?'

Maher said, 'It's not like that.'

Cain curled his lips into a sneer. 'So, go ahead and convince me.'

The Eagle Rock lawman wiped a slightly shaking hand across his round features. He said, 'This isn't easy for me, Cain.' He paused to lick clearly dry lips. 'The truth is, I'm in a fix . . . I took their money.'

Cain said, 'Why doesn't that surprise me? Whose money?'

Maher shook his sweat-speckled head. 'That's just it; I don't know. I got drawn into this private poker game. I always figured I was pretty good at cards, but I soon found out those boys, Powell, Allen, Stinger and Knot, were streets better. They led me on; letting me win small occasionally, so I would stay in, I guess. In the end they took me for three thousand dollars, my life's savings, and then they threatened to expose me unless I played along with what they'd got in mind. They said it would pay handsome if I did. I panicked, said yes and asked them what their boss wanted. They said if I did what he asked, and it was satisfactory, he would wipe the slate clean and I could go back to being an honest lawman again.' Remorse clearly in him, Maher added, 'I'll never be able to do that now, will I, Cain?'

Cain just stared his loathing.

Maher began pacing up and down the strip separating the cells from the outer wall. Once more he waved an arm. 'I get my orders through George Powell, mostly to stay low. As I guess you've already figured, I go through the motions, making folk believe I'm doing my job to the best of my ability.' Maher shook his head, his look expressing his remorse. 'Believe me, Cain, after ten years of clean policing I am not proud of what I am doing. You coming has made me see that. Dammit, I want out. I want to make amends.' He gripped the bars. His eyes suggested pleading now. 'Every man makes one mistake in his life, don't he, Cain?'

Cain felt as though he wanted to spit in the man's face, tell him to go to hell, but he also wanted to get out of jail. He said, 'OK. What have you got in mind?'

Maher appeared to relax slightly. He said, 'From what I hear you are one of the best there is. Out there you can act free. I will be able to feed you information. Truth is, Cain, I've got a feeling things are about to come to a head, people are going to get killed—'

'They already have,' Cain said, bitterly.

Regret filled Maher's bland features. 'Yeah. And I don't want any more innocent blood on my conscience.'

'You know something, Maher? You make me sick.'

Maher was now mopping his brow with a red polka-dot handkerchief. 'I'm walking a tightrope here, Cain. The town council are breathing down my neck. I'm sure they are beginning to smell a rat because I'm not producing any tangible results. That is why I arrested you and brought you in, thinking it would take them off my back for a while and make me look good. Now I realize I've been living a lie, trying to make believe this would go away soon and the range would settle down again.'

Cain studied the Eagle Rock sheriff. 'You realize turning me loose will make you even more suspect.'

'I'll handle it,' Maher said. 'What I want is for you to be out there, gathering information.' He waved a hand at the dark outside. 'The thing is, George Powell rides out of town every Monday to get his orders. I want you to trail him, find out whom he's getting his instructions from. Cain, I want to nail the bastard giving the orders. Dammit, I want to redeem what little self-respect I have left.'

Cain said, 'Why don't you trail Powell yourself? Is it because you haven't the belly for it any more?'

Maher said, 'No, it's because Jed Stinger, Bud Allen and Freddie Knot make sure I stay in town until Powell gets back.'

Cain nodded. The air in the cells was cloying and he could almost smell Maher's fear as he mentioned the hardcases. To be sure, Powell, Knot, Stinger and Allen could have that effect on a man, there was no denying that. He took a deep breath. 'OK, Maher, how are you going to work it?'

Maher's relief was tangible. He said,

'Like this. . . .'

CHAPTER ELEVEN

Cain topped out on the low bluff and eased the roan to a stop. He looked at the dark sky in which, as well as being full of stars that sparkled like diamonds, now hung a near-full moon. He touched the cross-hatched butt of the Colt Maher gave him before he left. The solid feel of the walnut handle secured in the holster at his right hip was reassuring. And the Winchester in the saddle boot by his right knee gave him further comfort.

He looked back across the silver range to the few dim lights that were still showing in Eagle Rock, a mile away in the silver-purple distance. He had left Maher on the cell floor, handcuffed and locked up. The two wounds he put in his head with his Colt were convincing ones. Cain grudgingly conceded it took a certain kind of guts on Maher's part to stand there and take the blows he gave him.

He looked at his pocket watch. The fingers told him it was past midnight. That made it Sunday. Before he beat Maher unconscious the Eagle Rock sheriff warned him that when Deputy Clem Frazer found him he would, of necessity, keep up his charade and avoid the suspicion of Powell and the others, and immediately organize a posse and head straight for the Flying W. Maher added, 'Take this advice, Cain: make for the hills and hole up until it's time to return to Eagle Rock to wait for George Powell to ride out Monday morning. When you've trailed him and we know who we're dealing with, we can take it from there.'

We? Cain formed his lips into a cynical smile. That was rich coming from a man who had sold out to grafters and killers.

With those thoughts Cain urged his roan off the butte top and headed for the Flying W. His best bet would be to seek out Medicine Bow Reynolds. The ex-mountain man, he assumed, would have a wide knowledge of this area and would know a place where he could hole up until the critical time on Monday.

Nine miles on he topped the gentle rise in the trail and looked down on the Flying W. The ranch house and outbuildings were dark and silent, their outlines etched in the moon's silver light. He walked his horse down the last of the trail's incline towards the cluster of buildings, standing silver in the moonlight. If Medicine Bow was back from his scout his pinto mustang must be in one of the barns, or one of the corrals. Cain checked the corrals first. No sign of the pinto.

At the first barn he came to he dismounted and

ground hitched the roan. He walked into its gloomy interior. Using the light from the moon, slanting in through the big doors, he saw that three beasts were stalled there. They moved restlessly when he entered. In the third stall he saw Medicine Bow's pinto. He relaxed. He guessed the old-timer must be in the bunkhouse sleeping.

To relax was a mistake. The attack came without warning. Cain saw the steel point of a big Bowie knife coming down towards his exposed neck, glinting in the moon's light. He moved with feline agility, his left arm swinging to beat away the descending blade, his right fist going in hard and low towards the advancing assailant's stomach. But his attacker was already dropping under the blow and rolling away to come up like a rubber ball before him, but at a safe distance. The cackling laugh that followed the moves was all too familiar.

'No use you doing that now, sonny,' Medicine Bow Reynolds said, 'I could have slit your throat twice over from ear to ear afore you even knew it.'

Rage swept through Cain. 'Damn you, Medicine Bow, you scared the living lights out of me.'

The ex-mountain man was still chuckling as he sheathed his big Bowie knife. 'Then you'll be more careful in future, won't you?' he said. 'Now, just what are you doing here? Lodge Woman said Maher took you into custody.'

'So he did.' Cain told him the story. When he was through Medicine Bow said, 'Well, I'll be damned. Are you saying Maher's getting himself some backbone?'

Cain said, 'I'm saying that's his plan.'

'But you ain't trusting it?'

'Not a lot of reason to.'

Medicine Bow rubbed his wizened right cheek. 'This George Powell and the other deputies that took you in, you say you know them?'

Cain nodded. 'Killers all,' he said. 'I traded lead with Powell once; put him in bed for a week; shoulder wound.'

Medicine Bow stared his surprise. 'You mean you didn't kill him?'

'I'm a lawman,' Cain said, 'not a killer. I have never deliberately killed any man when wounding was an option.'

'I've known lawmen who *like* killing people,' Medicine Bow said. 'They tell me it goes with the job.' The oldster spat tobacco juice and added, 'And d'you know something, sonny? I'm with them. You don't allow that kind of scum to live if you git the chance to send them to salvation. If you do, most times they come back and they won't be so up front next time; more like you'll get it in the back.'

Cain set his thin lips into a grim line. He remembered Jesus Lopez's failed bushwhack attempt. He fancied George Powell was equally capable of such an act, but Powell would be much more accurate in his attempt. But then Cain came to the opinion that George did have scruples of a sort. George liked to be up front, face his man. It was a matter of pride to him, the ultimate test of his skill. However, the others, Stinger, Allen and Freddie Knot . . . they were scrapings from the crapper. They would not give a damn how the killing was done.

Medicine Bow said, 'So, what do you figure on doing now?'

Cain pursed his lips. 'Can't stay here, that's for sure, in case Maher's plan is genuine. I'll have to get into the hills and hide out until Monday, then follow Powell, see what comes out of it. Might be just an elaborate ploy of Maher's to nail me, but then again it might be that Maher really wants to nail the bastard that got him into this fix in the first place.'

Medicine Bow cackled a laugh. 'Could be. And I know the very place you can hole up.' He screwed up his eyelids in enquiry and stared. 'By the way, you ate yet?'

'Some jail slop, is all,' Cain said. 'Given dogs better.'

'So get a meal into you,' Medicine Bow said, 'you'll need it and I figure you've got time. Then I'll take you to that place I know.' The mountain man looked up at the bandage Lodge Woman had put on Cain's wound. 'How's your head?'

Cain said, with some feeling, 'It hurts, dammit.' But he didn't carry the news of his miseries any further than that. He said, 'Did you manage to get anything on that bushwhacker yesterday morning?'

Medicine Bow's grizzled look turned sour. 'He's a real cunning son of a bitch, I must say. I followed him into hills, but lost him. Don't do that very often.'

'Wonder what those Blackfeet would've done about that?' Cain said making his sarcasm heavy and plain.

'Not a lot I fancy,' Medicine Bow admitted. Then added belligerently, as if he had just realized Cain's sarcasm, 'Are you trying to make a monkey out of me, sonny?'

Cain grinned. 'Wouldn't dream of it but it's just nice to know you're as fallible as the rest of us. What's the latest on Mrs Wilder?'

Medicine Bow said, 'Good is my belief. She woke around suppertime; took a little broth. Lodge Woman is pleased with her, so is Doc Mailer.'

'Well, that's good news, anyway,' Cain said.

Medicine Bow nodded fervently. 'She's as tough as old leather, that gal, yet sweet as a prairie flower. Let's go get those eats.'

The noise they made in the kitchen while preparing the meal soon woke the rest of the house. Lodge Woman came into the kitchen bug-eyed, looking mean and brandishing a carving knife. Ethan came next; but he must have popped out of a rear window and sneaked in through the common room and gathered up a shotgun on the way; a newer weapon than the one Bud Allen had shattered against a tree yesterday afternoon. Ethan held the shotgun level. He was clearly ready to use it as he sneaked in through the kitchen door, even though his eyes were still swollen with sleep. When Ethan saw who they were he relaxed and said, delighted,

'You got out.'

Cain grinned. 'I sure did, boy.'

'You escaped?'

'Something like that,' Cain said.

'No posse?' Ethan said.

'Not yet.'

'Gee,' Ethan said, adoration in his eyes, 'I knew you'd do it.'

'Go back to bed,' Lodge Woman scolded, 'and let Cain eat. Little Warrior not make big warrior if no sleep.'

'Aw, I wanna stay, Lodge Woman,' Ethan said.

The Crow woman waved the big knife in her hand. 'Go. Or Lodge Woman cut tail off Little Warrior if don't.' She hooted a laugh.

Grumbling, Ethan sulkily departed.

The intended meal cooked at last, Cain ate his ham and eggs, and flapjacks which he smothered with molasses. An hour later he and Medicine Bow were heading into the hills, victuals for two days packed into Cain's saddlebags, water canteen full. As they got into the higher country the air became keen, whitening the breaths of animal and human alike. An hour passed before Medicine Bow turned right. A mile on he skirted the bottom of a long escarpment, the base of which was screened by trees. Then he turned into a cave, hidden by a fold in the rock. Cain decided it was the perfect place for a man to hide and the high ground behind made an ideal place from which to scan the range, should he feel the need to do so.

Obviously pleased with himself Medicine Bow beamed at him. 'So, what d'you think?'

Cain nodded. 'Couldn't have found better myself, old-timer.'

'Sure you couldn't,' Medicine Bow said, pushing out his chest in pride and revealing his crooked-toothed grin. 'So, what d'you want me to do now, sonny? Get back to the ranch, look out for the boy and Mrs Wilder?'

Cain said, 'I'd feel a heap better if you did, Medicine Bow, though Lodge Woman seems capable enough.'

Medicine Bow squinted. After moments he said, 'You really care for that boy, don't you?'

'He's a spunky kid.'

'He's that all right,' Medicine Bow said. 'It's in the family. So, what's after you've trailed Powell?'

Cain shrugged. 'Don't rightly know, but by tomorrow night I should know more than I know now. Just stay close to the ranch until I get in touch.'

'How about the posse?'

'I figure you can handle that chore.'

Medicine Bow nodded in the cave's darkness. 'Sure I can.' He touched his battered slouch hat. 'Well, be seeing you, sonny.'

Cain raised a hand. He had been intending to bring up the subject ever since his first meeting with Medicine Bow, now his patience had finally been exhausted. 'One thing,' he said. 'I'm not "sonny", Medicine Bow. I'm a grown man.'

Medicine Bow cackled his laugh and raised his bushy brows. 'You aren't? Well, you are to me, sonny. Take it or leave it.'

Cain said, but feeling petty about it, 'OK. So how about "Old Crow" for you, huh? That suit?'

Medicine Bow shrugged, clearly unconcerned. 'It makes no difference to me. Some of the things I've been called you wouldn't believe.'

'Oh, I can believe all right.' Cain smiled a grim smile and nodded. 'Just watch your back, old-timer; those sons of bitches play for keeps.'

'Make sure you're watching yours,' Medicine Bow said. 'I ain't got to the age I am by not watching mine.'

The old-timer turned and led his horse out of the cave into the light of the moon. Once out there he paused and studied the heavens above the tops of the trees. After moments he turned his head and called, tersely,

'Come take a look at this, sonny.'

Curious, Cain walked to the cave's entrance and looked in the direction of Medicine Bow's point. Even though it was maybe ten miles away the thing the oldster pointed at was unmistakable, a faint angry orange glow above the treetops. Seeing it, Cain's gut clamped up. One thing was for sure; he knew fire when he saw it. 'We've got to go back and fast, Medicine Bow,' he said. 'My guess is that's the Flying W going up.'

Cain hurried back into the cave and retightened the girth on his roan, mounted and urged the beast out into the open night. Medicine Bow was already mounted and waiting for him when he got outside. No words passed between them as they set off, back down the trail.

After half an hour's hard riding Medicine Bow

held up his hand and reined in. Cain slithered his roan to a halt beside him, nearly crashing into the mountain man's wiry pinto. The skin on Medicine Bow's face was taut and riven with concern. 'Riders,' he said, 'and coming this way.'

Cain strained to hear. An interminable time seemed to pass before he heard the faint drum of hoofs in the night ahead. Now mildly astonished, Cain decided Medicine Bow must still have acute hearing.

Both swung off the trail, into the trees and waited. A minute later six men galloped into view and swept past them. Even though their outlines were indistinct Cain knew hardcase riders when he saw them. And it didn't take a huge leap of imagination to deduce it was they who had fired the Flying W, if that was what the glow in the sky signified. And it had to be. However, there was another possibility. It could be one of the homesteader's cabins in the next valley to the Flying W. But whether it was or it wasn't, Cain was now in a frame of mind which was telling him: choose what, he was going to chase those murderous bastards who just rode past them right down into hell if need be, particularly if more death had now occurred at the Flying W. He said, 'Go on to the ranch, Medicine Bow, I'm going after those sons of bitches to see where they hole up.'

Medicine Bow held up his hand, a crooked smile on his face. 'I've got a better idea, sonny: *you* go to the ranch. I'm the man to do the trailing. Got more know-how than you, even though I did fail to find the bushwhacker yesterday.'

Cain nodded. 'Makes sense, I guess. But don't tackle them on your own. Come back and get help.'

'Don't need your advice on that, sonny.'

With a quiet 'Ha!' Medicine Bow swung his pinto around and made tracks after the hard-riding hellions. Cain watched as the old-timer faded into the silver night, then raced his roan in the opposite direction.

CHAPTER TWELVE

Cain found that the closer he got to the Flying W the brighter became the glow in the sky. And with every mile-eating stride of his horse he found his anxiety mounting until it got to be a desperate ache. Worse, if the occupants of the house were caught napping they must surely have gone up with the flames.

He now found that all sorts of ghastly scenarios were flooding into his mind. He tried to push them into the background. He could usually divorce himself from the emotive side of such things, to enable himself to think rationally. But this time he found he was too deeply affected by what might have happened to Jane and Ethan Wilder and to Lodge Woman. They were people he could care about. Anxious determination surged through him. He drove the roan on.

Dawn was beginning to pale the sky when he pulled his roan, snorting and sweating, to a stop on a rise of ground half a mile north of the blazing ranch house.

His heart sank. It *was* the Flying W. Unmercifully he urged his horse the rest of the way to the doomed ranch house.

He was coming out of the cottonwoods by the river one hundred and fifty yards out from the ranch when the wall of heat hit him. Not only did he recoil, his roan also went back on its haunches – white-eyed and snorting, its natural fear of fire all too apparent. With hard cuts of the reins across its rump Cain urged the beast on. Now that he was as close as he dared to be to the fire he saw the barns were, as yet, untouched. He considered that entirely reasonable. The buildings were a good hundred yards from the house and the breeze was carrying the red-hot cinders in the opposite direction. Even so, a few sparks in the right places could easily create a new conflagration.

He dismounted and stared at the flames. They were consuming the ranch house with voracious appetite. So absorbed did he become that he soon found he was so close to the flames that he was finding it hard to breathe. The heat generated by the fire was sucking most of the air around into swirling vortices of sparks and flames that were leaping skyward before drifting southward on the night breeze.

He tightened his grip on the reins and did his best to hold the beast. He found the scene hypnotic. He became convinced nothing could possibly be left alive in there. The awful probability of it hit him like a physical blow. Jane Wilder, the boy, Lodge Woman, all gone? He attempted to close his mind; the thoughts were too awful to contemplate. But he found rage building in him, a passion to wreak terrible revenge upon the perpetrators of this terrible crime.

The voice from behind startled him. 'Mr Cain?'

Cain turned. The relief in him to see Ethan framed in the nearest barn doorway was almost overwhelming. After a moment's pause while he gathered himself he cried, 'My, God, Ethan, I thought you were dead!' His natural reserve dropped off him like a shawl. He let go of the reins on the roan and ran forward and hugged Ethan. 'Boy, am I glad to see you!'

Ethan disentangled himself slowly, Cain thought a little reluctantly, and said, 'Thank you, sir, but would you come into the barn? It is kind of urgent.'

Knots of concern bunched in Cain's stomach but he would not let his imagination run riot again. He followed Ethan into the barn's interior, made light by the fierce glow of the fire. He saw Lodge Woman was in the act of lifting the blanket-wrapped Mrs Wilder into the back of a cart with deep sides. A horse was already in the shafts. It was in harness and ready to go. Ethan's work? Cain now saw a thick bed of hay was spread on the cart's flat bottom. He ran forward and hopped up on to the cart's base, knelt and outstretched his arms.

'Is she alive, Lodge Woman?'

'Yes.'

'Pass her up to me. Easy now.'

Lodge Woman glared her indignation. 'I know easy,' she said. 'No need white man tell Lodge Woman . . . easy!'

As if crossly she raised her arms with Mrs Wilder's body lying across them. It would be quite a feat of strength for a man, Cain decided, but he was already of the opinion that Lodge Woman was a strong lady and would not be too strained by the lift. Proving it, Lodge Woman placed Mrs Wilder gently into his waiting arms.

Cain looked down into a face that was flour-pale. The pain showing in it was most marked in her sunken blue eyes. She met his grey stare. She said, her voice barely above a whisper, 'You're Jack Cain.'

'Yes, ma'am. Try to rest if you can.'

'We owe you so much,' she said.

'You owe me nothing, Mrs Wilder.'

'From what I have heard, that I can't believe.'

She sighed and closed her eyes. Cain laid her as gently as he could on the thick bed of hay, then he turned and looked down to see Lodge Woman was rummaging in her large bag. When her hand came out it was clasping a small bottle in which was brown fluid. She climbed up on to the plank seat of the flatbed with nimbleness that belied her large frame. Ethan climbed up with her. Lodge Woman waved a brown bottle in her hand. 'I gave to Jane Wilder just now to make her sleep,' she said. 'She will know nothing until we get to Eagle Rock. There, she has friends who will help her.'

Cain said, 'You think she can make the journey?'

117

'She make journey,' Lodge Woman said. 'I see to that.'

Cain said, 'Has there been a posse?'

'No posse,' said Lodge Woman. 'We go now.'

But just then Ethan yelled, 'Hold it.'

He jumped down and ran to the nearest barn wall, to a shotgun leaning there. He picked it up and turned to Cain. 'Pa always carried a spare. I picked it up as I ran from the fire.'

Cain remembered Bud Allen smashing the other one against the cottonwood shading the house yesterday. He nodded. 'Son, I reckon I would have gotten along real well with your pa.'

Ethan seemed to visibly swell with pride. He climbed up beside Lodge Woman. 'I guess he would with you, too, sir.'

Lodge Woman grinned. 'Big Warrior, huh, Cain?'

She was shrieking with laughter as she flapped the reins and coaxed the horse to walk on.

Cain stood back and watched them go gently up the west trail towards Eagle Rock. He watched them until they dropped below the brow of the rise and then led out the two horses remaining in the barn and tethered them way back in the trees. After that he unsaddled and rubbed down his roan and walked him around to cool before taking him to join the other horses in the trees.

When he returned he closed the big barn doors to stop sparks flying in. Even though they were being blown in the opposite direction there was always the possibility of a capricious change in wind direction.

Now he did the same with the other barn doors, picking up the two buckets by the door while doing so. There were no horses in the second barn.

The three horses in the nearest corral, he noticed, were restless. However, he decided they were in no danger there so he left them. But, with his roan being played out after his flat-out run to here, and this range being as dangerous as it was, as a precaution he saddled a frisky bay that looked likely to have bottom.

Now he stared into the morning sky. The as yet hidden sun was staining the heavens orange and yellow above the eastern hills, signalling its imminent appearance. The sight cheered him; things always appeared better in daylight. Nevertheless, he went down to the river, filled the two pails and carried them back to the barns and watched for any sign of fire starting on the outbuildings. There was nothing to be done with the house. It was a total loss, a glowing ruin, a pile of embers brightened only now and again in the caprices of the breeze.

All he could do now was wait for Medicine Bow.

CHAPTER THIRTEEN

Mid-morning, the sun baking hot, Medicine Bow came in from the north. His pinto's head hung low. It was clearly worn down by some hard riding. But, Cain noted, the old-timer appeared to be as sprightly as a year-old colt. Reaching him, the oldster climbed down and without the preliminaries said,

'Jane and the boy – are they all right?'

'Lodge Woman has taken them into Eagle Rock,' Cain said. 'They're fine, apart from Jane's wound, of course.'

Medicine Bow nodded. 'Well, that's good,' he said. 'But you'll never believe what I got to tell you.'

Too tired and smut-stained and now sitting with his back against the clapboards in the shade of the smaller barn, Cain said, 'Try me.'

'Those hardcases,' Medicine Bow said gleefully, 'they made straight for the Lazy R, Matt Wilson's place.'

Cain straightened, his tiredness falling off him like a shawl, his face hardening to set into grim disbelief

'The hell they did,' he said.

Medicine Bow grinned triumphantly. 'You figured them at the Lazy R were to be trusted, didn't you?' he said. 'I told you not to trust anybody, sonny, but did you listen?'

Cain stared with eyes made red by smoke. He growled, 'Because they went to the Lazy R don't mean Matt Wilson had anything to do with what's going on.' He raised dark brows. 'Now, his hired help on the other hand, Jim Struthers and Johnny Green . . . well, I guess the jury is out on them.' He climbed to his feet and eyed the oldster keenly. 'I'm heading up there to nose around a little.'

The oldster glared as if incredulous. 'What for? To get yourself killed?'

Cain said, 'I figure all isn't what it appears to be up at the Lazy R.'

Medicine Bow snorted. 'There you go agin,' he said. 'Appears to me Wilson and his two rannies are in this up to their necks. And you'd better believe it.' Then he added, as if it was an afterthought, 'Did the posse turn up?'

'No.'

Cain walked to the bay he'd saddled earlier, now tethered to the corral. He untied the rein and led it to the river. He filled his canteen and let the horse drink. Medicine Bow followed him on his tired pinto. While he waited the oldster screwed up his eyelids and said, 'You ate yet, sonny?'

Cain remounted the bay and looked down at the old man. 'No. I'll catch some fish in one of those

121

mountain pools. I won't starve.'

Medicine Bow grinned. 'Got some mountain man's chicken,' he said as if he was offering prize-winning cuisine.

Cain pulled a face. 'Squirrel?'

'Don't mock it,' Medicine Bow said. 'It's saved my life more'n once. It's all cooked and ready to eat. It's real dee-licious and sure as hell nothing to pull a face at. Sonny, you haven't lived until you've ate squirrel.'

With busy fingers Medicine Bow fumbled in the parfleche fastened to his saddle and handed over the meat. Cain took the mountain man's delicacy and pushed it into his saddle-bag – deciding that right now, anything was better than nothing. Even so, he said, 'How about you, old-timer? What are you going to do for eats? There isn't anything to eat here. It went up with the flames.'

Medicine Bow grinned his black-toothed grin. 'Don't worry about me, sonny,' he chirped. 'When I've seen things here are secure and the livestock have been tended to I'll be heading for town, to see if Jane and the boy are all right. As for food, they got eating houses in Eagle Rock, ain't they?'

'I reckon.'

Medicine Bow nodded. 'So what you asking for? Now, you got some sort of a plan before you go off half-cocked?'

Cain pursed his lips. 'Just hunches, I guess.'

Medicine Bow snorted and moved uneasily in the saddle. 'Hunches? Only a damn fool works on hunches.'

'They have paid off before,' Cain defended stubbornly.

Medicine Bow said, 'The hell they have. OK, go and get yourself killed, if that's the way you want it. See if I care.'

'I won't get killed. Have you got an alternative?'

'No, but that don't say I'm not working on it.'

'Well, I haven't the time to wait while you figure it out,' Cain said. 'I've got a feeling things are about to blow on this range, starting at the Lazy R. I want to be there when it happens.'

Medicine Bow sniffed. 'Well, I've warned you,' he said. 'It ain't no skin off my hide any more.' He waggled a finger. 'But I got a hunch you're going to need a bucketful of luck where you're going.'

Cain nodded. 'In that case, I'll wait for you in hell, you ornery old cuss.'

Medicine Bow hee-hawed a laugh. 'Go kiss my ass, sonny.'

Cain arched his brows. 'And risk catching rabies?'

At that crack, Medicine Bow chortled a laugh revealing his black teeth in all their crooked and tobacco-stained glory. Then he faded the grin. 'I'm being serious, boy. Watch your back real close; this ain't a game any more.'

Cain nodded and sobered too. 'It never has been, Medicine Bow.'

He turned the bay towards the hills.

CHAPTER FOURTEEN

After some hard riding he reached Wilson's place an hour past noon. It was deserted, or looked it. No smoke was rising from the yellow-stone chimney and there was no movement to be seen around the buildings.

He called, 'The house?'

He realized it was a damn fool thing to do, soon as he did it, but it was too late now.

However, he wanted to make things happen, even though there could be a modicum of risk attached to doing it. He found that the breathless pause he was now subjected to was similar to that of a crowd waiting for the hangman to pull the latch on the trapdoor so the victim could drop and swing.

'Well, howdy, Jack.'

Cain tensed up. The voice making the call was all too familiar and it was coming from the barn behind him. He leapt off the bay with the agility of a mountain cat, dragging his long gun out of its saddle scab-bard as he went.

He was sprinting and zigzagging the short distance to the house when the rifle from behind cracked, sending a squabble of echoes into the hills. Once, twice, three times lead sang close by. Lead hit the log walls of the house. One bullet splintered shards out of the door.

On reaching the stoop Cain dropped to the boards and rolled across them to the threshold of the ranch housethen plunged through into the living room beyond. He did not know what to expect. Coming up against the one cowhide settee he was about to get to his feet when Matt Wilson – it was definitely Wilson – yelled,

'Whoever it is, keep low!'

A handgun flared in the far corner. Noise followed. *Crack! Crack! Crack!* The ear-splitting din crashed into every corner of the room. It was so loud Cain didn't hear the hot lead as it hissed about his head.

He crouched down, aimed and fired at the shape behind the gun's flash. He was rewarded with a harsh cry, and then a sobbing sigh before the noises of pain faded into deadly silence.

But still Cain crouched, hardly daring to breathe, peering into the gloom of the room, his ears strain-ing to catch any further hostile movements. When he was reasonably sure the danger in the room was past he said,

'Where are you, Wilson?'

125

'Behind the curtain, on the bed. Is that you, Cain?'

'Yes.'

Still crouching Cain scuttled across the room. He tore the blanket screen aside. He saw Wilson was on the bed, trussed up like a chicken. He also noticed that the Lazy R rancher's face was badly bruised.

Cain quickly reached for his razor-sharp pocket-knife and slashed the bonds. While he was doing it he said, 'I want some answers, Wilson. Medicine Bow Reynolds said a bunch of hardcases I know stopped off here last night.'

'They did,' Wilson said bitterly, 'and I'm still getting over the surprise.'

Free of the bonds he sat up and began to rub life into his numbed limbs. 'But there's no time for that now,' he went on. 'We've still got trouble. There are two men in the barn, Johnny Green and Freddie Knot. I guess it was one of them that took shots at you just now.'

'Think it was Freddie Knot,' Cain said. 'I recognized his voice.'

Wilson stood up and began trying to stamp circulation into his deadened feet while swinging his arms windmill-like to do the same for his upper body. While he was doing so a tentative call came from outside,

'Jim? Did you get him?'

This time it was Johnny Green's voice. Cain whispered to Wilson, 'Who is that in the corner, d'you know?'

'Jim Struthers. By God, Cain, those two sure made

a fool of me. I never did figure them for hardcases.'

Cain said, 'Is there a back way out of here?'

'Uh-huh. Through the kitchen.'

'Know if it's covered?'

Wilson was stamping his feet now. 'Not that I know of, but I've been trussed up here most of the time.'

Cain nodded. 'Sit tight and wait here.'

Wilson stared. 'The hell I will. I've been confined here for eight hours, Cain, and beat up some. I want a piece of those sons of bitches.'

Cain said, 'All right, but get yourself loosened up first, and then arm yourself. After that, stay here because I figure I'll need covering fire. You may get your chance at them then.'

Wilson frowned. 'What are you going to do mean-time?'

'Try to get into the barn.'

Not waiting for an answer, Cain went through into the kitchen. There was a rear door. He lifted the latch and pushed because it clearly opened outwards. Through the chink he made he peered into the bright daylight and waited, listening. No shots came his way. A blackbird singing beautifully made an incongruous sound in this atmosphere loaded with tension.

Cain studied the vegetable plot, which was fifty yards or so from the rear door. A row of half-grown runner beans wilting in the heat offered limited cover until he could get into the willows and cotton-woods by the river.

A tingle of expectation ran up his spine. If he

127

could get into those trees yonder then he could work his way round, towards the rear of the barn. If he got even luckier he could perhaps get into the barn without being seen at all.

A rifle cracked three times but no lead hammered around him and he looked for other causes. He soon worked out that the noise was coming from behind him, within the house. It could only be Matt Wilson, trying to create a diversion. Confirming his assumption rifle fire crackled from the barn in answer and he heard glass break.

Wilson returned fire.

Cain dived out of the rear door, keeping low as he ran for the row of beans. Reaching them he travelled their length, then he sprinted across the green space between the vegetable plot and the trees. As he ran the exchange between Wilson, Green and Knot continued, rapping staccatos of noise into the blue sky. Cain picked his way through the tangle of greenery until he got to the edge of the trees. There he paused before the open ground between him and the barn and waited until Wilson released another string of shots. When Green and Knot replied he took a deep breath and scuttled across the open ground to the rear door of the barn.

He was halfway across when one of the ranch dogs rushed him. He kicked at it and felt firm connection, powerful enough to send the mutt squealing toward the house. Then he was through the big door and rolling over the thin layer of hay and dust covering the floor. He came up hard against the nearest stall wall. The horse in it was white-eyed and made restless by the deafening shooting that was going on. It kicked three times at the stall wall as Cain came up against it, the force of the blows vibrating the stout timber and jolting him. Fortunately none of the boards gave way. Now Cain waited and listened and tried to still his rapid breathing. He soon established that only one rifle was booming away in the barn, up in the loft. Cain licked his lips and wondered where the other shooter was situated.

He allowed his eyes to become accustomed to the intensified gloom in the interior of the barn, then he searched the whole area with alert eyes. No movement on the ground floor. The only movement was happening in the loft above.

Wilson began firing again from the house. Dust showered down from the barn roof as lead hissed in through the loft door and smashed through the shingles. The occupant of the loft quickly returned fire. One rifle only was there, Cain was almost sure of that. Even so it was still tricky, not knowing where the other hardcase was. Using the din of the shooting Cain took his chance on the other one being elsewhere and climbed the loft ladder two rungs at a time. By the time the firing eased off he was lying in the thick hay stacked on the loft floor. He stared hard at the man leaning against the boards to the left of the loft doors, rifle up and in the process of jacking in a fresh load. He soon realized that it was Johnny Green. He sighted up and said softly, hoping Freddie Knot was not close enough to hear, 'Throw down your rifle, Johnny, I've got you dead to rights.'

Green turned, a harsh gasp escaping his lips. He was lining up his Winchester when Cain's lead hit him in the sternum. Blood spurted and Johnnie's yell was harsh as he was smashed back by the impact of the bullet.

He hit the wall behind him with a thump, then he came forward. There he stood for some moments, holding his chest, coughing and swaying, blood gushing from his mouth. Cain's lead hit him again, in the solar plexus this time, and Johnnie reeled and toppled out of the loft door, his cries turning into a scream. A split second later Cain heard Green's body hit the ground below with a crumpled thud. After that, silence.

Using that silence Cain rolled twice and found a fresh position. There he waited and listened, while trying to shallow his breathing.

He held his rifle at the ready and waited for a target. There was still no movement below. He'd half-expected there might be. He wiped a shaking hand across his lips.

Knot, you son of a bitch, where are you?

Cain crept down the ladder and, after pausing to listen once more, he systematically searched the lower level. Apart from horses, there was nothing. Freddie Knot was not in the barn. The only conclusion he could come to was that Freddie must be in one of the two lean-to buildings that were each side of the barn, but which one? However, knowing Freddie reasonably well, Cain came to the opinion that Knot would be looking for a way out. Two on one were too high odds for an asshole like him to hang around for. Not only that, Cain had a good idea which way Freddie would go once he decided to make a run for it. On his sprint for the barn, he noticed that a horse was saddled and tethered back there in the trees. It must be Freddie's, for any hard-case worth his salt usually had a back-up plan lined up.

Cain climbed down to the barn floor and crept out of the rear door. He soon found a position where he could cover the two side buildings. Then came the voice he did not want to hear right now.

Matt Wilson called, 'You OK, Cain?'

Cain crouched, instinctively. He knew he should-n't answer the call. But then the idea came to him like a bolt out of the blue and it made a deal of sense to him. He croaked, 'Here, Matt.' Gasp. 'I'm hit bad.'

Tingling with anticipation now, he rolled to a fresh position and waited, trying to take in the rears of both lean-to buildings. A board broke out of the nearest one and, like a rat out of his hole, Freddie came at a run, firing his rifle in the direction Cain had made his call from moments ago. Cain felt grim satisfaction as he called, 'Wrong, Freddie; I'm over here.'

Knot's desperate cry rang across the open space. 'Oh, Jesus H Christ!'

The words barely out of his mouth, Freddie slewed around and fired from the hip, just a split second before Cain's lead took him in the brisket, causing crimson to blossom like a rosebud on his plain grey shirt before spreading rapidly. Cain heard Freddie's hastily fired shot buzz harmlessly overhead.

Cain watched Freddie go down, still on the run, staggering forward. He hit the ground nose first, his proboscis sliding through the grit and dust, which skinned it until he came to a standstill; then he lay still. Cain instinctively knew that Freddie would not be feeling pain any more. He was dead.

Cain stood up and commenced reloading the rifle. As he did Matt Wilson came out of the house and paced towards him, grinning.

'We whipped 'em real good, uh, Jack?' he said.

'Sure did,' Cain said. 'Now, what's the story, Matt?'

'How about I tell it over a cup of coffee, and something to eat?' Wilson said. 'I've been trussed up since before dawn this morning.'

Cain shrugged. 'Can't object to that.' He felt the tension of the last quarter of an hour fade and die within him. 'Lead on.'

CHAPTER FIFTEEN

Over a pile of fried ham and eggs, and coffee you could float a spoon in, Matt Wilson told all he knew. 'Seven of them came riding in hour before dawn, their horses all lathered up: Jed Stinger, Bud Allen, Freddie Knot, George Powell and three others, riding Bar H mounts. Two I recognized: Ned Sullivant and Jake Mole. They always side Hanson, until now it seems. The other guy I ain't seen before.'

Cain looked up, narrowing his eyelids as he stared over his forkful of ham. 'Bar H, Barton Hanson's outfit?'

Wilson nodded. 'It surprised me, too. They claimed they wanted fresh horses, theirs being all lathered up. They said they were riding posse for Sheriff Maher, after rustlers that hit King Laker's Floating L yesterday. I'd heard nothing about that, as I surely would have done. King Laker is my nearest neighbour. He'd want men to ride with him. Right off, I figured their claim did not ring true. Nevertheless, I got them their horses, deciding I

133

could be mistaken. However, it wasn't long before my doubts proved right because when I volunteered to go with them they trussed me up and said the hell I would; they'd got other plans for me. The implication in that was clear – to me anyway. I would not see another sunrise. But what truly took me by surprise was Struthers and Green joining them, just like they were old buddies from way back and had been expecting them. God dammit, I trusted those men, Jack.'

Wilson paused, raised brows and sighed. 'Well, they cooked breakfast like they owned the place. While they did, they talked about hitting King Laker's Floating L next. I wondered what the hell they meant by that. Then they said they would do the same to Laker what they done to the Flying W. Again, I asked them what they meant and Powell told me to shut my mouth or he would put me in a pine box right now.' Wilson's stare was now curious as it reached across the table. 'What did they mean by doing the same as they did to the Flying W, Jack?'

'They burnt the Wilder place to the ground last night.'

Wilson stared wide-eyed. He breathed, 'Oh, my God. Jane, the boy – are they all right?'

'They're OK,' Cain said. 'Lodge Woman has taken Mrs Wilder and the boy to friends in Eagle Rock for now.' Then Cain explained the circumstances leading to his being here at the Lazy R.

'And you thought I had something to do with burning out the Wilders?' Wilson said, as if made

134

incredulous by the implication.

'Dammit, what would you think, Matt? A gang like them running straight to your place after they'd done it?'

'The same, I guess.'

Cain scrubbed the bristles on his chin for some moments, then he said, 'OK, with three Bar H crew riding with that bunch of hardcases it's beginning to look as though Hanson is the one causing the trouble on this range. Going on what I know so far he's been suckering a lot of people with his good deeds in order to throw up a smoke screen. He had been king around here for so long he panicked as he watched the old way of life slipping away. He was not able to cope with it. Hence his campaign to get more land, to keep the sodbusters at arm's length, and not giving too much of a damn how he does it.'

Wilson shook his head as if to express his doubts. 'I can't bring myself to believe that, Jack. He's a lot of things, is Barton Hanson, but a rustler and killer he is not.'

Cain said, 'You're too soft, Matt. There are some cunning and ruthless bastards in this world and I'm thinking Hanson is one.'

Cain ate more ham dipped in egg yolk, then he said, 'You say they are heading for King Laker's Floating L?'

'That's what they said.'

'How far is Bear Paw Creek from here?'

'Twenty miles, but I figure we should ride into Eagle Rock and notify Sheriff Maher. He's the law

around here. We need to get a proper posse organized if it is Hanson, which I ain't saying it is.'

Cain said, 'Forget it, Maher's up to his neck in
what's going on. Whoever it is doing this, Hanson or
no, Maher's in their pay. He's admitted as much to
me.'

Wilson stared. 'The hell he has. Dammit, I always
had Maher down as straight.'

'Well, he isn't any more,' Cain said. 'Gambling
bets he can't pay, so he's paying for them by selling
his soul.'

The ex-lawman went on to tell of Maher's foolishness and of his wish to redress the wrongs he had
done. But Cain stressed his scepticism throughout.

When he finished Wilson said, hopefully, 'But if he
has come to his senses and he is acting like a lawman
again, we've got to find that posse he's sending out
and guide it to the Floating L.'

'It'll be too late,' Cain said. He mopped up the
remains of the egg and ham juices left on his plate
with a hunk of dark bread, put it in his mouth and
chewed it thoroughly before washing it down with
coffee. Then he said, 'Simple truth is, Matt, I don't
trust Maher. I figure we should get over to the
Floating L right now and warn Laker. I reckon we'll
have time, because it's my guess Powell and his hardcases won't hit the place before midnight. It isn't
their style to burn people out in the dayti—' The
faint drumming of many hoofs approaching silenced
any further talk Cain wanted to make. He met
Wilson's stare as it reached across the table.

'Can't think they're coming back.'

But he loosened his Colt anyway and got to his feet.

CHAPTER SIXTEEN

Wilson went to the rifle leaning against the wall with the door in it, the one he'd used against Green and Knot just now. Both men went to the door and stepped out on to the stoop. Close on fifteen riders were coming down the valley. They were still a quarter of a mile away and as yet unidentifiable. As they came on the horses grazing Lazy R grass scattered, then turned to stare at the intruders invading their quiet valley.

When the group got close enough to be recognized Cain saw that it was Barton Hanson heading them. The whole lot reined up before the ranch house, horses sweating and blowing. Hanson was burly and red-faced in the saddle. Without preliminaries he leaned forward and said, 'What the hell's going on, Cain?'

'Might ask you the same question.'

'All I know is the Flying W was razed last night and you went after the bastards that did it.'

'That's right.'

'So, dammit, tell it, man,' Hanson said impatiently.

Cain did, right up until now.

When he was finished the Bar H owner said, 'You say three of my men are with them – two whom I trusted implicitly, Sullivant and Mole? And they've gone on to the Floating L with the intention of burning it?'

Matt Wilson said, 'That's how I heard it.'

Hanson shook his head. 'It just don't make sense. What kind of people are they, for God's sake?'

Cain said, 'The same kind that killed Frank Wilder and his boy and their two hands, as well as doing the rustling hereabouts and the other killings.' Cain gazed directly at the rancher. 'You've been doing a deal of pushing yourself lately, Hanson, particularly at the Flying W. Could be it's you that's been doing it.'

Hanson stared, his look taking on the sheen of tempered steel. 'Why, that's crazy talk,' he said. 'I've been above board all the way. Sure, I've made no secret of the fact I want the Flying W, it abuts my range and has good water and Frank Wilder wasn't making the best use of it, in my opinion. But to burn and kill for it, that's not my style and never has been.'

'So you say,' Cain said.

'Damn it, I do say!' Hanson said.

Cain studied the big rancher for some moments before he said, 'Well, strange as it may seem, Hanson, I'm coming round to believing you.'

Hanson glared. 'Well, damn you, I don't give a

rat's ass if you do. What you've got is the truth. Now, what are we going to do about the Floating L?'

Cain said, 'Maher's supposed to have a posse out. Have you run into it?'

Hanson shook his head. 'No.'

'Have you talked with Medicine Bow Reynolds?' Cain said.

'In town,' Hanson said. 'That's who I got the story from and why I'm here.' Glaring fiercely now the rancher rocked in the saddle, as if impatient to be moving. 'Damn it, Cain, this is the first break we've had to get at these bastards. I'm near two hundred head down and I want justice. If those sons of bitches are heading for the Floating L, what are we waiting for?'

'Nothing, I guess,' said Cain.

The ride to the Floating L was made with grim faces, even though they went through green hills and valleys that were pleasant to the eye. They passed two homesteads. As the second one was passed Hanson said, grumpily, 'I tell you, Cain, this range is getting too damn crowded. A man don't have *room* any more.'

Around mid-afternoon beeves began to show aplenty on the grassy hills and Matt Wilson announced that they were on Floating L range and had been for quarter of an hour. Around five o'clock Cain saw black, oily-looking smoke billowing up beyond the trees on the distant horizon. Cain set his jaw into a grim line. Seemed his guess they would not strike until dark was in ruins. Riding beside him Matt

Wilson said, 'It's got to be the Floating L, Jack.'

Without prompting the pace of the posse picked up. As they got closer the crackle of gunfire, faint at first, became sharp and clear and increasingly threatening the closer they got to the pillar of smoke. Hanson shouted in Cain's direction, above the drumming of hoofs.

'Sounds as though King's making a fight of it.'

'Can't argue with that,' Cain said. He held up his hand to bring to a halt the posse, of which he was in the lead, along with Wilson and the Bar H owner. He said, 'We've got to think about this, Hanson.' He turned to Wilson. 'Matt, you know the lie of the land up there. Explain.'

'The ranch buildings sit in a shallow basin and—'

A yell came from the brow of the hillside beneath which they had come to a halt. The call stopped Wilson's flow. Rifle fire began to crackle and the ridge became alive with smoke and gun flashes. One of Hanson's riders went down and lay still. The rancher shouted, 'Get into cover, men.'

Meantime, Cain stared around him, the coolness he'd always displayed under fire coming to his aid once again. He could see copses of pines were scattered all the way up the hillside. He yelled, 'Head for the largest copse, men, and find cover.'

Amid more ragged volleys from the ridge, in which another Bar H rider swayed in the saddle but kept his seat, they eventually piled into the cover of a small wood. Soon return fire began to spear from amongst the pines and there was a mad scatter on the ridge to find better cover.

Though Cain gave the order he did not follow them into the trees. He turned to Matt Wilson, who was beside him. 'Follow me down the slope, Matt!'

Once out of range he turned and counted the rifles blazing out from the ridge, then he looked speculatively at the sky. Soon it would be dark and, knowing Powell and the bastards who must be with him, his best bet was they would use the night to make their escape . . . but only if they figured that the situation here was getting too hot to handle.

Assuming he was right, a plan quickly formed in Cain's mind. He turned and assessed the ground around him. They were in a small valley. Cottonwoods and willows lined the river that ran along its bottom not fifty yards to their left: good cover if he ever saw it. He stared at Matt. 'Tell me about the rest of the layout at the Floating L, Matt.'

Wilson did.

Cain nodded. 'OK, I'm going to scout out the situation up there, see what they've got around the back. Go join Hanson and explain what I'm doing and tell him to keep in cover until I get back.'

He did not wait for Wilson to answer. He dug heels into the bay and raced it across the fifty yards to the river, crossed it and melded into the cover of the cottonwoods and willows that were lining it.

Grim-faced now, he headed up the valley. He needed to get to the rear of the Floating L. What would come after that he did not know. He just felt he needed to do it so the situation could be assessed fully. But the movement in the bushes to his left had him swinging round, his Colt up and ready to fire.

What the hell?

CHAPTER SEVENTEEN

Medicine Bow Reynolds came out of the greenery. It was as though the old-timer and his mustang just grew out of the ground. Cain stared. 'Dammit, you should know better than come up on a man like that!'

Medicine Bow spat brown juice into the river. It seemed to be a gesture of slight contempt. 'If you're heading for where I think you're heading, sonny,' he said, 'I can fill you in on that situation and save you the trouble. But first off, there's eight hooligans on the ridge up there—'

'Already know that. You're wasting time.'

Medicine Bow narrowed his eyelids, his stare inno-cent-looking and surprised. 'You do?' He sniffed. 'Yeah, well, figured you might; don't take you for a complete fool. What you don't know is – and what you're figuring to find out, I guess – Powell and what's left of his boys and the three Bar H crew are

144

the other side of the ranch house. But the icing on the cake, sonny, is they have a stranger with them and I figure he's the man we're looking for.'

Keen anticipation ran through Cain's whole being, like a bloodhound coming on to a scent. 'The hell he is? D'you know who it is?'

Medicine Bow stared more contempt. 'Dammit, he wouldn't be a stranger if I did, now would he?'

Cain brushed aside Medicine Bow's scorn. 'Have you seen King Laker and his crew?'

'They're holed up in the barn. Two hands are dead, far as I can make out, but they are making a real fight of it.'

Cain found himself rapidly assembling the knowledge he now possessed. On the face of it, the odds were in favour of Hanson's fifteen-man crew. And with the added help of Medicine Bow Reynolds, Matt Wilson and himself Cain figured they now held the advantage, even though the hardcases on the ridge did have the benefit of the high ground.

Medicine Bow interrupted his train of thought with the astonished comment, 'Dammit, it's Maher and his posse!'

Medicine Bow was pointing to the brow of the valley behind them. Cain estimated there must be ten in the posse and it was clearly composed of townsmen. They made a sweating, red-faced bunch in bowler hats and dusty suits in various stages of discard on account of the ferocity of afternoon heat. Some carried rifles, others Colts; two held shotguns. They obviously came prepared for a fight.

Medicine Bow growled, 'Well, I'm not hanging around here to talk to that son of a bitch. See you soon, sonny.'

Cain stared. 'Where you going? We need you.'

Reynolds spat juice. 'You'll see me when I'm ready.'

He kicked flanks and melded into the greenery giving Cain no chance to answer. He turned and waited for Maher.

When the Eagle Rock sheriff came up close and eased down his blowing roan along with the rest of the posse Cain said, 'I won't ask where you've been, Maher, but my guess is your mystery man, the man you say has been blackmailing you but you don't know, is at Laker's ranch right now, come to watch the fireworks. Well, I figure it isn't fun for him any more because we've got him boxed, or will have.' Cain narrowed his eyelids and curled a cynical smile across his thin lips. 'So, it's make your mind up time, Sheriff. Are you going to join him in the fray, seeing as you have been jumping to his tune, or are you going to stay here? I must warn you, though, you won't get six yards from here if you try to join him.'

Maher nodded. 'OK, Cain, you've made your point.' He waved a hand at the posse. His look now became frank. 'They know, Cain. I've come clean and on account of my past record, they are willing to review my position once this mess has been cleared up.' Maher now flickered a glance across the ridge protecting the hardcases; it was still alive with brisk gunfire, as was the copse in which were Hanson and his men. 'You must know the situation here; what do you want us to do?'

Cain weighed up the situation. According to Matt Wilson the Floating L ranch house and its outbuildings sat in a shallow basin beyond the bend in this valley. He ran his gaze across the ridge's length. First priority: the ridge's flanks needed to be covered. He wanted the lot of these killing bastards. But he guessed the real killers ... George Powell, Jed Stinger, Bud Allen and maybe Ned Sullivant and Jake Mole, were down at the ranch house with the son of a bitch who had stirred up all this trouble.

He looked at Maher and pointed at the ridge. 'Those flanks need to be closed, Maher. You can handle that?'

The sheriff of Eagle Rock nodded. 'The posse is composed of capable men, Cain, some of them war veterans. But how about the Floating L's rear? That needs to be taken care of.'

'I agree—'

Medicine Bow came riding in, fast. He slithered his pinto a halt beside Cain and said, heavy urgency in his voice, 'The birds are flying the coup, sonny.'

So that was where the old devil had been. Cain stared at the oldster for a moment and then turned to Maher.

'Close up those holes, Maher,' he said. Then he swung his bay. 'OK, let's get to it, Medicine Bow.'

After five minutes' hard ride in the cover of the cottonwoods they swung around the back of the smouldering remains of the Floating L ranch house. They found Hanson's man, Ned Sullivant, and a stranger they didn't know dead, probably the other Bar H rider. But no Jake Mole. Had that rat-faced bastard made a run for it early and was now miles away from here?

Cain now turned his gaze on to the Floating L barn. King Laker and what was left of his crew were now concentrating their fire on the ridge that Hanson and his men were contesting.

Cain turned to Medicine Bow. 'Which way did they go when they lit out, old-timer?'

'Thought you'd never ask. This way.'

Medicine Bow put his pinto into a run west. Half a mile on they found Jed Stinger dead on the trail. Cain could only assume that one of Laker's men had got him as he rode out. That left George Powell and Bud Allen and the bastard who'd ordered all this mayhem. Two miles on they rode down into another small valley sprinkled with cottonwoods, sycamore and aspen. In the middle of it the trail split. One rider had continued west, the other two had contin- ued north.

Medicine Bow drew rein. His narrowed gaze engaged Cain's. 'If we're going to get them all,' he said, 'we'll have to split up.'

Cain nodded. 'Take the single rider, Medicine Bow, but remember, whoever it is will be a killer; don't take anything for granted or try anything fool- ish.'

Medicine Bow stared his disgust. 'I fought the

148

Sioux and Blackfeet, sonny, *real* hard bastards they were. You'd be advised to look to your own hide.'

Medicine Bow lit out to the west.

A half-smile on his lips, Cain picked up the trail north and followed it patiently. Being new-grown grass it was not a difficult thing to do. But being so obvious there should be trickery ahead, he was sure of that, particularly if it was George Powell he was trailing. The other rider, he decided, must be the mystery man. Whether he would choose to stand was another matter and Cain decided he would not waste time on speculating about it now for the group of rocks up ahead looked suspicious and he was on clear ground. He was an open target. And if he knew George Powell at all, this would be a gift sent from hell and that man would not waste it.

Do the unexpected!

Excitement sparkling through him, Cain put his bay into a run, while concentrating his gaze on the jumble of rocks ahead. In the last rays of the evening sun he saw the dull glint of steel flash for a second in the rocks. He figured it was not quartz. This was not quartz country.

He pulled his Winchester and jacked off three shots at the flash. Rock splintered and the whine of ricochets howled into the arc of evening sky. In anxious reply, shots crashed their noise out from the rocks. It was the boom of a high-calibre rifle. The kind of rifle that would leave the type of gaping wound that had been inflicted upon Jane Wilder.

As never before, the desire to kill descended upon Cain.

He veered his horse's run and spurred the bay around the west side of the rock mass and – only briefly, he knew – out of the line of fire. There he dropped off the bay at a run and carrying his rifle sprinted for the rocks and not a moment too soon. The big weapon was booming again. Jets of earth squirted up around him and once more it was a thankful man who finally gained the cover of the rocks.

Breathing hard, Cain licked his dry lips as silence clamped down like a shroud over the rock formations. After moments, breath regained, he eased his way through the grotesque jumble of red rock, occasionally pausing to listen. He had a general idea where the shots were coming from, but he did not head directly that way; he came in at it from an oblique angle.

It was a mistake.

The boom of the rifle came from his left and spurts of rock splinters, some chipping out flesh on his face, stung like angry bees. Blood trickled down his face. He swung the Winchester and levered off three shots, then moved again and waited, crouched in the rocks, his nerves strung up as tight as the string on an Arapaho warbow. The silence stretched into minutes.

Cain looked anxiously at the sky. Dammit, he was going to lose the light. But so was his ambusher, who he suspected must be George Powell.

Proving it, the harsh call startled him. 'Cain!'

He spun, his gut knotting up. He saw Powell was thirty feet to his right, standing on a huge rock, as large as life. Well, George had never lacked confidence and he always did like to look a man in the eye when he was about to kill him.

'Been nice knowing you, Jack!' Powell was warbling.

Full of desperate anxiety, Cain rolled in the confined space between the rocks, sighting up as Powell unleashed his charge of lead.

Cain felt something pull powerfully at the top of his shoulder but it did not deflect his concentration, for Powell was framed amid his own gun smoke and silhouetted in the light of the orange sun behind him.

Cain jacked off two shots. Powell yelled and jerked like a puppet on strings. Shock and surprise was on his face as he toppled off the rock, to land with a bony crump at the base of it.

Cain ran the few feet that separated them, another bullet jacked into the breech ready to fmish the bastard off. But when he reached Powell he looked down into dead eyes that were looking back at him mockingly.

He stared for moments with mixed feelings. Then he said, 'So long, George. I can't say it's been nice knowing you, but you were always a game bastard.'

Then, dismissing the gunsel from his mind, Cain turned his attention to the wound in his shoulder. The bullet had grazed the top of his collarbone. It was bleeding and it would be painful but it was not life threatening.

He made his way back to the bay. He took a clean shirt from the saddle-bag. It would do to pad the wound until he could get proper medical aid. Fifteen minutes on he was back in the saddle and using the last light of the day as he followed the trail leading from the rocks; obviously made by a single rider . . . *the rogue card in this game of death?*

As the last of the day snuffed out, panoplies of stars spread across the big arc of sky. He pressed on, ignoring the pain that throbbed in his shoulder. He was bent on one thing: to get this matter cleared up once and for all. Some bastard was out to kill him, that was for sure, and he wanted to know who that person was. For these kinds of mysteries hung about like shadows. They were always threatening and in the background and needing solving so that a man could move free and not have that cold tingle sprinkling his backbone at each suspicious sound in the dark night. Or have the uncertainty of not knowing what awaited him every time he stepped out of his door to live, breathe and rejoice at that prospect of engaging with the next new and vital day.

It was near nine o'clock, according to his pocket watch, when he spotted the fire ahead. It was amid a copse of trees. He frowned, but he also felt cautious optimism. Did his quarry have such confidence in George Powell's assassination abilities to camp so close to the bushwhack site and then wait, expecting the job to be done and for Powell to join him when it was?

And why was Jack Cain the target? That still remained the biggest mystery.

Cain decided boldness was his best option. He rode right into camp but was careful to come up from the rear. The fellow remained seated by the fire. He did not even turn round. But a rasping sensation of cold amazement sawed across Cain's gut as recognition came to him. He knew that back; he knew what little of the profile he could see framed in the flickering firelight.

Still without looking the fellow said, 'Did you get it done, George?'

'Guess not, Nate.'

There was stiffening in the backbone. Nate Creed spread out his arms, his finger ends curled in like claws.

He gasped. 'Cain?'

'Reckon so.'

Cain dismounted, ground-hitched the bay, and sat on a rock opposite the Still County rancher who had once been his good friend. Nate Creed stared across the snapping fire, straight up into his eyes. He held Cain's glare for some moments, then sighed and dropped his shoulders. He said, 'Well, I half-figured you would be too good for him.'

Cain said, 'I guess you are at the back of all that's been going on here, uh? Why, Nate, wasn't Still County big enough for you?'

'You saw to that with your meddling and killed my boy doing it!'

'Jacob brought it on himself and you know that. And are you saying you were behind the trouble in Still County until I stopped it? Always had the feeling I never did get to the bottom of things in that fracas.'

Nate Creed stared across the firelight, his eyes like two bullet heads. 'You've never known real ambition, have you, Jack? The kind of ambition that drives a man on? The kind of ambition that knows no boundaries, knows no laws, only the laws that bring him money and power and the influence those two things generate? I could have done a lot of good in Still County, Jack, but for your damned interference.'

Cain stared and said, but it was more of a sneer, 'Sorry to spoil your party.' Then added, 'Did you send your boy against me?'

Nate Creed's return glare was ferocious as he breathed, 'What kind of a man do you think I am?'

Cain said, shaking his head, 'You really don't know, do you? You've got blood on your hands, man – women's blood, men's blood; good men and good women who have never done you harm. On top of that there's the heartache and misery your behaviour has brought. But the terrible thing is, Nate, you don't realize it.'

Creed scowled and waved a dismissive right hand. 'To make a good omelette, Jack, you have to break a few eggs. Half of those people were, or are, wasting their land. They deserve to be run off, killed, if they resist. I've no sympathy. This is the land where the strongest win. I'm strong.'

Cain said, 'Did you send Jesus Lopez to get me?'

'A bungling idiot,' Creed said, 'a wanderer. I knew him, used his skills with horses in Still County. Like a lot of people, he has a weakness: he likes lots of money in his pocket. To cut a long story short, when you left Still County I had you trailed. When you bought in on what was going on here I immediately decided you were not going to ruin my plans a second time.' Dismissively waving his hand again Creed added, 'Lopez was handy so I used him to get rid of you.'

Cain said, 'Powell, did he kill Frank Wilder and his son and their two hands? And did he shoot Mrs Wilder and make a try for me?'

'Yes. On my orders.' Nate Creed's cold blue eyes came up, glittering in the light of the campfire. 'This isn't over, Jack. There are plenty of other guns I can hire. And, despite what you've done to my family and me I still have a grudging admiration for you. Ride on for Montana and I'll forget this.'

'Not in a coon's age,' Cain said.

Moments ago Cain became aware of faint movement behind him and it was no critter. Lithe as a mountain cat he rolled away from the firelight, drawing his Colt as he did so. Jake Mole was silhouetted in the fire's flickering glow. He looked startled. His hand was coming up, holding his Colt.

Cain fired from the hip and Mole was flung back by the impact of the bullet. Blood began spurting from the former Bar H man's throat and he started threshing about, choking on his own gore. Cain paid him no mind. His concentration was now fully on Nate Creed.

Creed was tugging at the Colt caught under the flap of his broadcloth coat, housed in a shoulder holster. Cain shot him between the eyes; there was no mercy in him.

POSTSCRIPT

Barton Hanson forgot his ambitions to buy out the Wilder place after some persuasive talks with Jack Cain. With help from the rancher and settlers on the range they rebuilt the Flying F ranch house and King Laker's Floating L. Matt Wilson went on to breed some of the finest horses the county ever produced.

After dealing with Hanson, Cain stayed on at the Flying W at Jane Wilder's sickbed request. After four months of Lodge Woman's herbal brews and careful nursing Mrs Wilder recovered to eventually live a long and happy life with Cain as her second and devoted husband.

Medicine Bow Reynolds, who turned west at the parting of the trails during the chase, tracked down and killed Jed Stinger. He did not scalp him, as he said the Blackfeet would have done. After that, Medicine Bow stayed on at the Flying W for the next two years. He eventually left to live out the rest of his life in the Arizona sun; to toast his rheumatics, he said.

Ethan grew up to be a respected US marshal, climbing to the highest echelons of that respected profession. He was also blessed with a sister and another brother, sired by his best friend and step-father Jack Cain.

Things can work out fine occasionally.